PEN

THE MA

'Miss Read', or in real life
profession who started writing after the Second World War, beginning with light essays written under her own name, mainly for *Punch*. She has written on educational and country matters for various journals, and worked as a script-writer for the B.B.C.

'Miss Read' is married, with one daughter, and lives in a tiny Berkshire hamlet. Her hobbies are theatre-going, listening to music and reading. She is a local magistrate and, of course, a manager of the local village school!

'Miss Read' has published numerous books, including *Village School* (1955), *Village Diary* (1957), *Thrush Green* (1959), *Fresh from the Country* (1960), *Winter in Thrush Green* (1961), *Miss Clare Remembers* (1962), an anthology, *Country Bunch* (1963), *Over the Gate* (1964), *Village Christmas* (1966), *The Howards of Caxley* (1967), *Fairacre Festival* (1968), *News from Thrush Green* (1970), two books for children, *Hobby Horse Cottage* and *Hob and the Horse-bat*, and The Red Bus Series for the very young. Her most recent books are *Farther Afield* (1974), *Battles at Thrush Green* (1975), *No Holly for Miss Quinn* (1976), *Village Affairs* (1977), *Return to Thrush Green* (1978), *The White Robin* (1979) and *Village Centenary* (1980).

Many of 'Miss Read's' books are published in Penguins including a special omnibus edition entitled *Chronicles of Fairacre*.

'MISS READ'

THE MARKET SQUARE

DRAWINGS BY HARRY GRIMLEY

PENGUIN BOOKS

Penguin Books Ltd, Harmondsworth, Middlesex, England
Penguin Books, 40 West 23rd Street, New York, New York 10010, U.S.A.
Penguin Books Australia Ltd, Ringwood, Victoria, Australia
Penguin Books Canada Ltd, 2801 John Street, Markham, Ontario, Canada L3R 1B4
Penguin Books (N.Z.) Ltd, 182–190 Wairau Road, Auckland 10, New Zealand

—

First published by Michael Joseph 1966
Published in Penguin Books 1969
Reprinted 1970, 1976, 1977, 1981, 1983

—

—

Made and printed in Great Britain by
Hazell Watson & Viney Ltd,
Aylesbury, Bucks
Set in Linotype Granjon

To
Olive and Philip
with love

CONTENTS

PART ONE

PART TWO

Part One

1. A June Morning

IT had been raining in Caxley, but now the sun was out again. A sharp summer shower had sent the shoppers into doorways, and many of the stallholders, too, from the market square, had sought more shelter than their flimsy awnings could provide.

Only fat Mrs Petty remained by her fish stall, red-faced and beaming through the veils of rain that poured from the covers above the herring and hake, the mussels and mullet. She roared a few rude and derisory remarks to her more prudent neighbours sheltering across the road, but the rain made such a drumming on the canvas, such a gurgling in the gutters, that it was impossible to hear a word.

It spun on the stones of the market square like a million silver coins. Office windows were slammed shut, shopkeepers braved the downpour to snatch in the wares they had been displaying on the pavement, and even the pigeons took cover.

It ended as suddenly as it had begun, and people emerged again into the glistening streets. The pigeons flew down from the plinths of the Corn Exchange and strutted through the shining puddles, their coral feet splashing up tiny rainbows as iridescent as their own opal necks. There was a fresh sweetness in the air, and Bender North, struggling out of his ironmongery shop with a pile of doormats in his arms, took a great thankful breath.

'Ah!' he sighed, dropping his burden on the pavement from which he had so recently rescued it. He kicked the mats deftly into a neat pile, and, hands on hips, breathed in again deeply. He was a hefty, barrel-shaped man and had been feeling the heat badly these last few days, and his much-loved garden was getting parched. This refreshing shower was welcome. He surveyed the steaming awnings in the market with an approving eye.

No one – not even Bender himself – could quite remember how he had come by his odd name. He had been christened Bertram Lewis thirty-five years earlier at the parish church across the market square. Some said that as a youth he had liked to show off his outstanding muscular strength by twisting pieces of metal in his great hands. Others, who had shared his schooldays at the old National School in Caxley High Street, maintained that he was so often called upon to 'bend over for six' that some wag had decided that 'Bender' was the perfect name for this boisterous, lusty rebel against authority. Whatever the reason, now long forgotten, for dubbing him thus, the name stuck, and if any stranger had asked in Caxley for Bertram North, rather than Bender North, he would have been met with blank countenances.

Bender watched the stallholders resuming their activities. The man who sold glue was busy smashing saucers deftly, and putting them together again with equal dexterity, while a crowd of gaping country folk watched him with wonder and amusement. Fat Mrs Petty shook a shower of silver sprats from the scale-pan into a newspaper. Tom and Fred Lawrence, who ran a market garden on the outskirts of the town, handed over bunches of young carrots and turnips, stuffed lettuces into already overcrowded baskets, weighed mounds of spring greens, broccoli, turnip tops, and potatoes, bawling with lungs of brass the while. This was Caxley at its best, thought Bender! Plenty of life, plenty of people, and plenty of money changing hands!

'A mouse trap, North,' said a voice behind him, and the ironmonger returned hastily to his own duties. He knew, before he turned to face his customer, who she was. That clipped authoritative boom could only belong to Miss Violet Hurley, and it was a voice that commanded, and unfailingly received, immediate attention.

'This way, ma'am,' said Bender, standing back to allow Miss Hurley to enter. He inclined his broad back at a respectful angle, for though the lady might buy nothing more than a mouse trap, she was a sister of Sir Edmund Hurley at Springbourne, and gentry needed careful handling.

'Sharp shower, ma'am,' he added conversationally when he was again behind the broad counter confronting his customer. She stood there, gaunt and shabby, her scrawny neck ringed with a rope of beautiful pearls, her sparse grey locks sticking out from under her dusty feathered hat like straw from beneath a ruffled hen.

'Hm!' grunted Miss Hurley shortly. Her foot tapped ominously on Bender's bare boards. This was not the day for airy nothings, Bender realized. Miss Hurley was in one of her moods. She should have found him in the shop, not dallying outside on the pavement. He reached down a large box from the shelf behind him, blew off the dust delicately, and began to display his wares.

' "The Break-back", "The Sterling", "The Invincible", "The Elite",' chanted Bender, pushing them forward in turn. He took a breath and was about to extract more models from the bottom of the box but was cut short.

'Two "Sterling",' snapped Miss Hurley. 'Send them up. Immediately, mind. Book 'em as usual.'

She wheeled off to the door, her back like a ramrod, her bony legs, in their speckled woollen stockings, bearing her swiftly out into the sunshine.

'Thank you, ma'am,' murmured Bender, bowing gracefully. 'You ol' faggot!' he added softly as he straightened up again.

He wrapped up the two jangling mouse traps, tied the

parcel neatly with string, and wrote: 'Miss V. Hurley, By Hand' with a stub of flat carpenter's pencil.

'Bob!' he shouted, without looking up from his work. 'Bob! Here a minute!'

Above his head the kettles, saucepans, fly swats, and hob-nail boots which hung from the varnished ceiling, shuddered in the uproar. A door burst open at the far end of the shop, and a black-haired urchin with steel spectacles fell in.

'Sir?' gasped the boy.

'Miss Hurley's. At the double,' said Bender, tossing the parcel to him. The boy caught it and vanished through the open door into the market square.

'And wipe your nose!' shouted Bender after him. Duty done, he dusted the counter with a massive hand, and followed the boy into the bustle and sunshine of the market square.

The first thing that Bender saw was Miss Violet Hurley emerging from Sep Howard's bakery at the corner of the square. Sep himself, a small taut figure in his white overall, was showing his customer out with much the same deference as the ironmonger had displayed a few minutes earlier. He held a square white box in his hands, and followed the lady round the corner.

'Taking a pork pie home, I'll be bound,' thought Bender. Howard's raised pork pies were becoming as famous as his lardy cakes. There was something particularly succulent about the glazed golden pastry that brought the customers back for more, time and time again. Pondering on the pies, watching the pigeons paddling in the wet gutter, Bender decided to stroll over and buy one for the family supper.

He met Sep at the doorway of the baker's shop. The little man was breathless and for once his pale face was pink.

'Been running, Sep?' asked Bender jocularly, looking down from his great height.

'Just serving Miss Violet,' replied Septimus. He paused as though wondering if he should say more. Unwonted excitement nudged him into further disclosures.

'She's as good as promised me the order for Miss Frances' wedding cake,' he confided. 'You could've knocked me down with a feather.'

He hurried into the shop in front of Bender and scurried behind the counter. Beaming indulgently, Bender followed with heavy tread. The air was warm and fragrant with the delicious odours from steaming pies, pasties, scones, fruit cakes and a vast dark dish of newly-baked gingerbread, glistening with fat and black treacle.

Mrs Howard was serving. Her hands scrabbled among the wares, dropped them in paper bags, twirled the corners and received the money as though she had not a minute to lose. Howard's bakery was patronized by the stallholders as well as the town people on market day and trade was brisk.

'A pork pie, please, Sep,' said Bender. 'A big 'un. I'll pay now.'

He watched the baker inspecting the row of pies earnestly and felt amusement bubbling up in him. Same old Sep! Dead solemn whatever he was doing! Why, he'd seen him at school, years before, studying his sums with just that same patient worried look, anxious to do the right thing, fearful of causing offence.

'They all look good to me,' said Bender. 'Any of 'em'll suit me.' Lord love Almighty, he thought, we'll be here till Christmas if old Sep don't get a move on!

The baker lifted a beauty with care, put it in a bag and came round the counter to give it to Bender.

'I'll open the door for you,' he said. 'So many people pushing in you might get it broken.'

'That's what you want, ain't it?'

'You know that,' said Septimus earnestly.

They found themselves in the doorway, Sep still holding the bag.

'I should be able to let you have the last of the loan at the end of the week, Bender,' he said in a low voice.

'You don't want to fret yourself about that,' answered Bender, with rough kindness. 'No hurry as far as I'm concerned.'

'But there is as far as I am,' said Sep with dignity. 'I don't like to be beholden. Not that I'm not grateful, as you well know –'

'Say no more,' said Bender. 'Hand us the pie, man, and I'll be getting back to the shop.'

The baker handed it over and then looked about the market square as though he were seeing it for the first time.

'Nice bright day,' he said with some surprise.

'Expect it in June,' replied Bender. 'It'll be the longest day next week. Then we'll start seeing the trimmings going up. They tell me the Council's having bunting all round the square and down the High Street.'

'Well, it's over sixty years since the last Coronation,' said Septimus. 'About time we had a splash. It seems only yesterday we were decorating the town for the old Queen's Diamond Jubilee!'

'Four years ago,' commented Bender. 'That was a real do, wasn't it, Sep? Beer enough to float a battleship.'

He dug his massive elbow into the baker's thin ribs, and gave a roar of laughter that sent the pigeons fluttering. Septimus's white face grew dusky with embarrassment.

'Ah! I was forgetting you'd signed the pledge,' chuckled his tormentor. 'You'll have to change your ways now the war's over and we've got a new King. Be a bit more sporty, and enjoy life, Sep! Once we've crowned Edward the Seventh on June the twenty-sixth you'll find Caxley'll start fizzing. Keep up with the times, Sep my boy! You're not a Victorian any longer!'

Muttering some excuse the little baker hurried back to his customers, while Bender, balancing the fragrant white parcel on his great hand, strode back through the puddles and the pigeons, smiling at his secret thoughts.

Septimus stepped down into his busy shop, trying to hide the agitation this encounter had caused. Why should a brush with Bender always give him this sick fluttering in his stomach? He had known him all his life – been born within a few yards and in the same year as this man. They had shared schooldays, celebrations, football matches, and all the life of the little town, but always the rift remained.

'You're nothing but a yellow coward,' Sep told himself disgustedly, stacking hot loaves in the window. 'Why can't you meet Bender man to man? He's no better than you are. His joking's only a bit of fun, and yet you are all aquake the minute he starts to take a rise out of you.'

He watched Bender stopping to speak to one of the stallholders. He saw his great shoulders heave with laughter as he turned again and vanished into the murk of his shop. At once Sep's tension relaxed, and he despised himself for it. Did Bender ever guess, he wondered, how much he affected other people?

Take this morning, for instance, thought the little baker, threading his way through the customers to the comparative peace of the bakehouse at the back. Bender could never have known how much he would upset him by talking of Queen Victoria like that. The death of the old Queen had shaken many people. Septimus Howard was one of them. She was more to him than a reigning monarch. She was the mother of her people, a symbol of security, prosperity and order. She offered an example of high-minded principles and respectable family life. She was the arch-matriarch of a great nation. And Septimus loved her.

He loved her because, in his eyes, she had always been right and she had always been there, safely on the throne of England. His father and mother, staunch Methodists both, had revered the Queen with almost as much piety as the stern God they worshipped, thrice every Sunday, at the Wesleyan Chapel in the High Street. Their children, with the possible exception of flighty Louisa, shared their parents' devotion.

Septimus knew he would never forget the shock of that terrible news which Caxley had heard only a few months before. It was a dark January afternoon, the shop was empty and Sep had been engaged in cutting wrapping paper ready for the next day's supplies. He saw Tom Bellinger, the verger of St Peter's across the square, hurry up the steps and disappear inside. Within three minutes the tolling bell began to send out its sad message.

Sep put aside his knife and went to the door.

'Who's gone?' he asked Sergeant Watts, the policeman, who was striding by.

'The Queen, God rest her,' he replied. For one moment they stood facing each other in silence, then the policeman hurried on, leaving Septimus too stricken to speak. He made his way to the quiet warmth of the bakehouse and sat down, stunned, at the great scrubbed table where he made the loaves, letting the tears roll unchecked down his cheeks. Not even when his father had died had he felt such a sense of loss. This was the end of life as he knew it. An England without Queen Victoria at its head seemed utterly strange and frightening.

Septimus disliked change. He was not sure that he wanted to be an Edwardian. Something in that new word made him as nervous as he felt in Bender's presence. He suspected that the new monarch had some of Bender's qualities; his gusto, his hearty laugh, his ease of manner and his ability to know what the other fellow was thinking. The new King loved life. Septimus, his humble subject, was a little afraid of it. He mourned Victoria, not only for herself, but for all that she stood for– a way of life which had lasted for decades and which suited him, as it had suited so many of his fellow countrymen.

At the time of the Queen's Diamond Jubilee in 1897, a fund had been opened in Caxley to provide a lasting memorial of this outstanding reign. Septimus Howard was one of the first contributors. He gave as much as he could possibly afford, which was not a great deal, for times were hard with him just then, and his fourth child was about to be born. But he was proud to give, and prouder still when he stood in the market place, later that year, and watched the fine drinking fountain, surmounted by a statue of Her Majesty, being unveiled by the Mayor in his red robe of office.

Now four years later, the statue stood as an accepted landmark in Caxley. Children played on its steps and drank from the four iron cups chained at each corner of the plinth supporting the sovereign. The cheerful rogue who sold bunches of roses in the market, sprinkled his wilting blooms with water from the great basin, and Mrs Petty dipped in an enamel mug and sloshed the contents over the fish stall before the afternoon customers arrived. The fountain was much appreciated, and Caxley folk often wondered how they had managed so long without it.

But to Septimus, the statue above it gave greater comfort. He looked down upon it every morning whilst he shaved at the mahogany stand in the bedroom window. The view, it is true, was shrouded a little by the lace curtains which modestly covered the windows, but that morning glimpse of Victoria meant much to the little baker.

And now, on this hot June morning, with excitement mounting everywhere at the thought of the Coronation so soon to come, Sep looked again at the small bronze crown just showing above the flapping awnings in the market square. The shop was more crowded than ever, the heat was intense, the noise deafening, but Sep had found new strength.

Bender's visit, the thought of the money he owed him, the staggering news from Miss Violet about the order for her niece's wedding cake, suddenly seemed to matter less. Somehow, Sep knew, he would be able to face everything. Surely, to have spent all the thirty-five years of one's life with the example of the Queen to follow must give a chap enough strength to recognize and perform his duties, and to welcome her son without trepidation!

He squared his shoulders, dropped six sugary buns into a paper bag and handed it down to a waiting urchin.

'Threepence, my dear,' said Mr Howard the baker briskly.

All fears had gone, and Sep was himself again.

2. *The Norths at Home*

'NASTY accident over at Beech Green,' observed Bender to his wife Hilda that evening.

'What's happened?' asked Mrs North, putting down the vast pair of trousers, belonging to her husband, which she was mending.

'Some youngster – forgotten his name – fell off the top of one of Miller's hay wagons. Young Jesse Miller was in the shop this afternoon. He told me. Just been up to see the boy at the hospital. Wheel went over his shoulder, so Jesse said. Pretty bad evidently.'

'People have no business to allow children to get into such danger,' said Hilda North firmly. 'Asking for trouble.'

Bender laughed.

'What about our kids and the boat?' he replied.

'I'm always saying,' retorted his wife, 'that I don't hold with it. One of these days one of ours will be drowned, and you'll only have yourself to blame, Bender.'

'You fret too much,' said Bender good-naturedly. 'They can all swim. What's the point in having a fine river like the Cax at the end of the garden if you don't have a bit of fun on it?'

His wife made no reply. This was an old argument and she had too much mending to get through to waste her energies that evening. Bender turned back to his desk and silence fell again in the sitting-room.

It was a vast, beautifully proportioned room on the first floor. It ran across the shop below and had three fine Georgian windows overlooking the market square. During the day, the room was flooded with sunlight, for it faced south, but now, at nine o'clock on a June evening, the room was in shadow, the gas lamp hissed gently in its globe on the ceiling, casting its light on Hilda's needlework and the great back of Bender bending over his crowded and untidy desk as he wrote out some bills.

Through the window before him he could see the last of the stallholders packing up. Two men with brooms were brushing up cabbage leaves, pieces of paper, orange peel, and all the market day débris. The setting sun shone pinkly on the upper parts of the buildings at right angles to Bender's shop. Septimus's bedroom window gleamed like a sheet of gold as it caught the last hour or so of dying sunlight. Soon its light would be doused by the creeping shadow of St Peter's spire, which lengthened and climbed steadily up the west-facing shops and houses in the market square, like some gigantic candle snuffer.

It was quiet in the great room. Bender hummed now and again and shuffled his papers, a faint squeaking from Mrs North's well-laced stays could be heard when she moved to reach more thread from her work-box, and occasionally the whirring of a pigeon's wings as it returned to roost on the parapet of the Norths' roof.

At last, Bender pushed his papers carelessly to the back of the desk, anchored them with a small ancient flat-iron, and threw himself, with a contented grunt, into the arm chair opposite his wife.

'Why you use that ugly old thing for a paper-weight I can't think!' commented Hilda. 'What's wrong with the glass one we bought at Weymouth last summer?'

'Too fiddle-faddle,' answered Bender easily. 'I like my old dad's flat-iron.'

He began to fill his black Turk's head pipe with deliberation. The fragrance of strong tobacco crept about the room as the great china tobacco jar beside him stood un-stoppered. His big roughened fingers worked delicately at his task, and when the tobacco was tamped down exactly as he liked it

Bender took a long paper spill from a vase on the mantelpiece and, crossing to the gas lamp, held it above the globe until it caught fire.

Soon the room was wreathed in clouds of blue smoke, the stopper was replaced and secured with a massive brass screw on the top of the tobacco jar, and Bender was prepared for his evening relaxation.

He looked about him with pleasure. His possessions– the dearest of them still busy with her mending – gave him enormous quiet pride. He liked the grey watered silk wallpaper that had been new when they married twelve years ago, and was now comfortably grubby. He liked the sofa, the armchairs and the two prim little occasional chairs, flanking the sofa, all upholstered in good dark red velvet. He liked the heavy mahogany sideboard, richly carved, and crowded permanently with silver, china, bronze, as well as the ephemera of daily living such as letters awaiting answers, bundles of knitting, indigestion tablets, and spectacle cases.

There was something particularly satisfying too about the octagonal mahogany table which stood always by his armchair. His niece had worked the pink and red silk roses on the black satin mat, which stood plumb in the table top's centre. It was a handsome piece of work for a twelve-year-old to have accomplished, thought Bender approvingly, and she had finished it with a splendid silky fringe a good two inches in length. She had also made a companion piece which ran the length of the top of the walnut piano against the wall. Its beauties were somewhat hidden by Hilda's group of naked china cherubs and the two great nautilus shells which stood on each side of them, but the little girl's workmanship was much admired by those waiting to sing, one elbow lodged nonchalantly on the black satin runner while the accompanist was propping the music on the music rest.

No doubt about it, thought Bender puffing dreamily, it looked rich, and he liked richness. His eye roamed indulgently over the crowded room, the wide wooden picture frames, the chenille curtains looped back with fine brass bands, and the cases of dried grasses and sea lavender on the corner brackets near by. It looked the sort of place a prosperous tradesman deserved, and he was indeed prospering. His wandering gaze came to rest upon his wife, now snipping busily at a frayed lining. It was to Hilda, as much as anything else, that he owed his growing prosperity. She worked as hard – harder maybe, thought Bender candidly – than he did himself. When they were first married they had thought nothing of being in the shop at seven in the morning until nine or ten at night. Somehow she had still managed to clean and cook, to sew and knit, and to bring up the family to be as industrious as she was herself.

She was a small plump young woman, fair-haired, and grey-eyed, with a pink button of a mouth, not unlike the old queen in her younger days. The bearing of three children – the first tragically stillborn – had thickened her waist a little, but tight lacing kept her figure still trim and shapely. To Bender's delight, she loved bright colours, unlike many matrons of her own age and times, and tonight she wore a lilac print frock decorated with bands of purple braid. Beneath its hem Bender could see her small black shoes adorned with cut steel buckles.

She looked across at him quickly, aware of his gaze.

'Where was Jesse Miller off to?' she inquired, harking back to the snippet of news.

'Never asked him. Beech Green, I should think. He'd done his buying at market and seen the young chap in hospital.'

'More likely to have gone up to my home,' commented Hilda. 'Pa says he's been calling to see our young Ethel lately.'

'Why not?' said Bender, smiling lazily. 'He must be twenty-odd, going to have a good farm with his brother Harold, when the old man goes aloft, and I reckon Ethel'd be lucky to get him.'

'He's a bit wild, they say,' responded Hilda, letting her mending fall into her lap and looking into the distance.

'Who's "they"?' asked Bender testily. 'There's too much gossip in Caxley. People here mind everyone else's business but their own! Makes me sick!'

He tapped out his pipe irritably.

'I'd sooner see young Ethel wed to Jesse Miller,' he continued, 'than that waster Dan Crockford she's so sweet on! What's the future in painting pictures for a living? He wants to get down to a job of work and keep his paint brushes for the week-end. If I were Dan Crockford's father I'd chuck him out to fend for himself! No, our Ethel's better off as a farmer's wife, and I hope she'll have the sense to see it!'

'Well, well, well! Don't get ratty about it,' replied his wife equably. 'They're both old enough to know their own minds, and it's time Ethel settled down.'

She rolled up the trousers briskly, and stood up, picking ends of thread from the lilac frock with quick pink fingers.

'Let's take a turn in the garden before we go up,' she said. 'It's still so hot. I wonder if the children are feeling it? Bertie was tossing and turning when I went up just now.'

Bender lumbered to his feet.

'They'll be all right. The girl's up there if they want anything. Come and look at the river, my dear.'

She led the way down the staircase, pausing on the landing, head cocked on one side for any sound from above. But all was silent. They made their way through the little parlour behind the shop, and the great shadowy store shed which housed ironmongery of every shape and size, and smelt of paint and polish, tar and turpentine, and the cold odour of stone floors, and cast iron girders.

It was almost dark when they emerged into the garden. It was small, with a brick wall on each side, and a lawn which ran gently down to the banks of the Cax. The air was soft and warm, and fragrant with the roses which climbed over the walls and the white jasmine starring the rustic arch which spanned the side path. Bender's shop might be villainously untidy and his desk chaotic. His neighbours might scoff at his muddles there, but here, in the garden, Bender kept everything in orderly beauty.

The river, lapping at the bank, kept his soil moist even in the blazing heat of such a spell as this. The Norths had always been great gardeners, and Bender was one of the best of his family. He looked about his trim flower beds with pride.

A rustic seat stood close by the river and here the two sat, while the midges hummed and a bat darted back and forth above the water. Sitting there, with the peace of the summer evening about them, was pleasantly relaxing.

'Where does it go?' asked Hilda suddenly.

'What? The river?'

'Yes. Does it go to London?'

'Must do, I suppose. The Cax runs into the Thames about fifteen to twenty miles east, so they told us at school, if I recall it aright.'

'Seems funny, doesn't it,' said Hilda dreamily, 'to think it goes past our garden and then right up to London. Sees a bit of life when it gets there. Specially just now with the streets being decked up for the Coronation. It said in the paper today that no end of royalty have arrived already, and troops from Canada and Australia for the procession. Wouldn't it be lovely if we could go, Bender? I'd give my eye teeth for a sight of the Coronation, wouldn't you?'

Bender smiled indulgently at this womanly excitement.

'I'm quite content to watch the Caxley flags and fairy-lights next week,' he replied. 'Maybe have a drink or two, and keep a lookout for the bonfire up on the beacon. We'll give the King a good send-off, you'll see, without having to traipse to London for a bit of fun.'

His wife sighed, and was about to speak when she caught sight of something white glimmering in the shadows of the fuchsia bush, and went over to investigate.

'What is it?' asked Bender following her. Hilda was turning a little white yacht in her hands.

'It must be the Howard children's,' she said. 'Bertie asked them over to bathe after tea. They've forgotten it. Another trip to make, running after them.' There was a tartness in her tone which did not escape her husband's ear.

'Only child-like,' he commented easily. 'I'm glad Bertie thought of asking them. They've nowhere to play in their baker's yard. Not much fun there for kids this weather.'

'Oh, I don't mind the *children*,' said Hilda, a trifle pettishly. 'And Septimus is all right.'

It's strange how she always calls him Septimus and not Sep, as everyone else does, thought Bender. These little primnesses about his wife never failed to amuse him. The fact that she could never bring herself to ask the butcher for belly of pork, but always asked delicately for stomach of pork, delighted Bender perennially.

'It's Edna I can't take to,' went on Hilda. 'Try as I might there's something about her – I don't know. I can't think what Septimus saw in her, respectable as he is.'

She had picked a tasselled blossom from the fuchsia bush and now tossed it petulantly into the darkening water. Bender put a massive arm round her plump shoulders.

'Are you sending your contribution to the Coronation decorations?' he asked jocularly, nodding towards the floating flower. 'It should get to Westminster in a couple of days.'

'And keep fresh in the water,' agreed his wife, smiling. Bender congratulated himself on his success in changing the subject. Once embarked on the ways of Edna Howard, Hilda could become mighty waspish for such a good-natured wife.

At that moment, the quarters chimed across the market square from St Peter's, and Hilda became agitated.

'Gracious me! That must be half past ten, and I've not had a word with Vera! You lock up, Ben, while I run upstairs.'

She flitted away from him across the grass, as light on her feet as when he first met her, thought her husband watching her depart.

He turned for a last look at the Cax before following her into the house. The twilight had deepened now into an amethyst glow. The river glided slowly round the great curve which swept eastward, shining like a silver ribbon beneath the darkening sky. Say what you like, Bender told himself, Caxley in June took a lot of beating! Let the whole world flock to London to see the King crowned! This was good enough for Bender North!

He picked up the toy boat from the rustic seat. Tomorrow he'd take it back himself to Sep's youngsters. No point in upsetting Hilda with it.

He left it on the bench in the store shed, where his eye could light on it in the morning, locked and bolted the doors of his domain, and made his way contentedly to bed.

3. Consternation in Caxley

THE bunting was going up all over England, under the bright June skies. In the villages round about Caxley there was a joyful bustle of Coronation preparations. At Fairacre School an ambitious maypole dance was causing heartache to the infants' teacher there, and bewilderment to the young fry who lumbered round and round, ribbons in hand, weaving the biggest and brightest tangle ever seen in the history of the parish.

On the downs above Beech Green a great pile of faggots was outlined against the clear sky, waiting for a torch to be plunged into its heart on June the twenty-sixth. The blaze would be visible from four counties, the old men told each other, and some said that they could remember their fathers talking of the blazing beacon, on the self-same spot, which had celebrated the end of the Napoleonic Wars.

The drapers in Caxley were running short of red, white, and blue ribbon, and the little saddler in West Street was surprised to find that his horse-braid in these three colours was in demand, not only for plaiting manes and other orthodox uses, but also for decorating trestle tables, oil lamps in village halls, and even for tying patriotic children's hair now that all the ribbon had been snapped up by early shoppers.

The market square at Caxley blossomed like a rose. Strings of fairy lights were festooned round the sides of the square and tubs of red and white geraniums, edged with lobelia, flanked the steps of Queen Victoria's plinth. Less happy was the arrangement of red, white and blue ribbons radiating from an erection on the crown of Her Imperial Majesty. Like the spokes of a wheel they formed a circular canopy rather like that of Fairacre's maypole in readiness for the troublesome dance. Septimus Howard looking down on it from his bedroom window, cut-throat razor in hand, thought it looked as garish as the market place at Michaelmas Fair. He overheard an old countryman observe to his crony as he surveyed this centrepiece:

'Fair *tawdry*, 'ennit, Ern?' and, privately, Sep heartily agreed with him.

It was on the evening of the twenty-fourth that the blow fell. King Edward had been stricken with appendicitis. He was dangerously ill. The Coronation would have to be postponed. This was no time for rejoicing, but for earnest prayer for the King's recovery. There were those who said that was doubtful – but, as Bender North said stoutly – there are dismal johnnies everywhere at such times, and they should not be heeded.

It was Edna Howard who had brought the dire tidings to North's shop, and thus added yet another misdeed, in Hilda's eyes, to those already committed. The shop was closed, but Bender was still tidying shelves and sweeping odd scraps from counter to floor with a massive hand.

Hilda stood at the door, and watched Edna Howard advance across the square, with that lilting gait, and proud turn of her dark head, which irritated Hilda so unaccountably. Edna was a tall woman, large bosomed, and long-legged, with a mass of black silky hair. Her eyes were quick and dark, starred with thick black lashes, and with an odd slant to them which told of gipsy blood. For Edna Howard had been a Bryant before her marriage, the only girl among a tribe of stalwart boys. Her mother had been a true gipsy, who had left her wandering family when she married a doting farm labourer and settled near Fairacre to produce a family of her own.

There was something foreign and wild about Edna

Howard which stolid Caxley inhabitants could not understand. In the country, memories are long, and despite Edna's respectable marriage, her industry in the shop and home, and her devoted care of her children, Edna's exotic streak was the first thing to be mentioned when the worthies discussed her.

'Plenty of the ol' gyppo about that 'un,' they said. 'Remember her ma? Used to come round with a basket o' pegs not so long ago.'

Edna knew very well the sort of remark that was made behind her back, and gave no hint of caring. She dressed in colours that were gaudy in comparison with those worn by her sedate neighbours. Sometimes she knotted a bright silk scarf about her throat, gipsy fashion, as though flaunting her origin, and on her wrist she jangled a coin bracelet which had once been her gipsy grandmother's.

Two other qualities added to Edna's colourful character. She possessed a thrillingly deep contralto voice and she could play the banjo. For some reason, Caxley approved of the first gift but was somewhat shocked by the second. Occasionally, Mrs Howard was invited to sing at charity concerts, by ladies who were organizing these affairs. The fact that she was an accomplished banjoist was known, but ignored, by the organizers. 'Sweet and Low', rendered by Mrs Septimus Howard to the decorous accompaniment on the pianoforte by the Vicar's son was permissible in the Corn Exchange. Edna Howard, let loose with her banjo, might prove a trifle vulgar, it was felt.

How meek little Septimus had ever managed to capture this wild bright bird was one of the mysteries of Caxley history. That Edna Bryant was 'one for the boys' was well-known. She could have picked a husband from among dozens who courted her from the time she was fifteen. Perhaps Sep's wistful shyness was the main attraction, contrasting so strongly with her own vivid confidence. In any case, the marriage had flourished, despite much early head-shaking, and Edna Howard was outwardly accepted in Caxley life.

Hilda unbolted the shop door and let Edna in with a polite smile. Bender's was considerably more welcoming. He liked a handsome woman, and he didn't much mind if Hilda knew it.

'Come on in, Edna,' he shouted heartily. She rewarded him with a warm smile and a provocative glance from under her dark lashes which Hilda did her best to ignore.

'Just brought the pattern I promised you,' said Edna, holding out an envelope. 'It turned out fine for Kathy, and you only need a yard and a half.'

'Thank you,' replied Hilda. 'You shouldn't have bothered, specially leaving the children in bed.'

This was a shrewd blow, and was not missed either by Edna or Bender. Under the surface solicitude, the sentence managed to imply parental neglect and to draw attention to the fact that Edna had no resident help in the house to mind her offspring, as Hilda herself had.

'Sep's there,' said Edna shortly. She put up a dusky thin hand to brush back a wisp of hair. The coin bracelet jingled gaily.

'You heard the news?' she continued. There was a hint of excitement in her casual tone.

'What about?' said Bender, coming forward. He was frankly interested to know what was afoot. Hilda assumed an air of indifference. Really, local tittle-tattle did not interest her! She blew some dust from a box of screws with an expression of distaste.

'The King!' said Edna. 'They say he's been took bad, and the Coronation's off.'

Hilda was shaken from her lofty attitude. Her mouth fell open into a round pink O.

'You don't say! The poor dear! What's the matter?'

'The King!' echoed Bender, thunderstruck. 'You sure this is true?'

'Gospel! Had it from Lord Turley's coachman. He told him himself. Lord Turley's just got back from London on the train.'

This was news indeed.

'But what about all this 'ere?' spluttered Bender, waving a large, dirty hand at the bedecked market place.

'And the parties? And the concerts and all that?' echoed Hilda, all dignity forgotten in the face of this calamity.

'And what about poor Sep's baking?' retorted Edna. 'He's got a bakehouse chock full of iced cakes, and sausage rolls, and a great batch of dough ready for the buns. I tell you, it's ruination for us, as well as bad luck for the King!'

Bender's face grew grave. He knew, only too well, the narrow margin between Sep's solvency and his business downfall. He spoke with forced cheerfulness.

'Don't you fret about that, Edna. It won't be as bad as you think. But do the Council know? Has the Mayor been told? And what about the vicar? Ought to be summat done about a service pretty sharp.'

Edna did not know. Her cares were all for the King's condition and her husband's set-backs.

'I'll be getting back,' she said, putting the paper pattern on the counter. There was a hint of sadness now in her downcast countenance which stirred Hilda's conscience.

'No, Edna, don't you worry,' she said, with unaccustomed gentleness. 'It's a sore blow for everyone, but the one who's suffering most is poor Queen Alexandra, and the Family too. There'll be another Coronation as soon as the King's fit, you'll see, my dear, and then all our troubles will be over.'

She walked with Edna to the door and let her out, watching her walk back across the square beneath the fluttering flags. Hardly had she closed the door when one of the Corporation's carts, drawn by two great carthorses, clattered to the centre of the market square. Two men jumped down and began to remove the ribbons which bedizened the statue of the old Queen. At the same moment the bell of St Peter's began to ring out, calling all parishioners to prayer.

'Let's go, Bender,' said Hilda suddenly.

Without a word, Bender removed his overall, and accompanied his wife aloft to fetch jacket, hat, and gloves.

Within three minutes, the Norths with other bewildered Caxley folk, crossed the market square, fast being denuded of its finery, and, with heavy hearts, entered the sombre porch of the parish church.

From a top floor window, high above the ironmonger's shop, young Bertie North looked down upon the scene, unknown to his parents.

It is difficult to go to sleep on summer evenings when you are eight years old and put to bed firmly at seven o'clock. Bertie resented this early bed-time. Just because Winnie, two years his junior, had to go then, it seemed mighty unfair to expect a man of his advanced age to retire simply because it saved trouble for Vera, the girl. He did not make a fuss about the matter. Bertie North was a peace-loving child, and did not want to upset Vera, the fourteen-year-old country girl from Beech Green, who worked hard from seven in the morning until the North children were in bed at night.

But the injustice rankled. And tonight, as he stood at the high window in his cotton night-shirt, he felt even more resentful, for there, far below, he could see the two Howard boys. They were hopping gaily about the statue, watching all the activity of taking down the ribbons and fairy lights. Bertie had seen them bob down behind the stone plinth to hide from their mother as she made her way home from visiting his own parents.

They weren't made to go to bed so early! Of course, thought Bertie reasonably, they were much older than he was; Jim was twelve, and Leslie was ten. His particular friend, Kathy, who was only seven, had to go to bed when her little brother did, just as he did. This crumb of cold comfort went a small way towards consoling the boy gazing down at the enviable freedom of the older children.

The bell stopped ringing, and the everyday noises could be heard once more. The clop of the horses' great shaggy hooves, as they moved across the cobblestones of the market square, mingled with the screaming of swifts round the spire of St Peter's. Behind him, in one of the back bedrooms looking across the river Cax, he could hear Vera singing to herself as she darned socks.

There were four little bedrooms at the top of the tall old house. Bertie and Winnie had one each overlooking the square. Vera had another, and the fourth was known as 'the boxroom' and was filled with the most fascinating objects, from a dressmaker's model, with a formidable bust covered in red sateen and a wire skirt, to a dusty pile of framed portraits of North ancestors complete with cravats, pomaded locks, and beards.

These old be-whiskered faces intrigued young Bertie. He liked to think that he belonged to the same family; that they too had once been his age, had run across the market square with their iron hoops as he did, and floated their toy boats on the placid face of the river Cax. His father and mother had been patient in answering his questions, and he already had an idea of his respectable background. Brought up in a community which recognized the clear divisions of class, Bertie knew the Norths' place in the scale and was happy to be there.

The Norths were middle class. They were respected

tradespeople, church-goers and, best of all, comfortably off. Bertie was glad he was not in the class above his – the gentry. Their children were sent away to school or had stern governesses. Their fathers and mothers seemed to be away from home a great deal. It would not have suited Bertie. Sometimes a passing pang of envy shot through him when he saw his betters on ponies of their own, for Bertie loved horses dearly. But there was always the sturdy little cob that pulled Uncle Ted's trap in the High Street, and on this the boy lavished his affection.

He was even more thankful that he did not belong to the class below, the poor. The people who lived in the low-lying area of Caxley, called 'The Marsh', were objects of pity and a certain measure of fear. Respectable children were not allowed to roam those dark narrow streets alone. On winter nights, the hissing gas lamp on the corner of the lane leading from the High Street to the marsh, simply accentuated the sinister murk of the labyrinth of alleys and small courtyards which were huddled, higgledy-piggledy, behind the gracious façade of the Georgian shop fronts.

Other people – far too many of them for Bertie's tender heart – were also poor. He saw them in his father's shop, thin, timid, unpleasantly smelly, rooting in their pockets or worn purses for the pence to pay for two screws, a cheap pudding basin, or a little kettle. They were pathetically anxious not to give any trouble.

'Don't 'ee bother to wrap it, sir,' they said to Bender deferentially.

'It don't matter if it's a mite rusty,' said another one day. ''Twill be good enough for I.'

It seemed strange to the listening boy, his head not far above the counter, that the poor whose money was so precious, should be content to accept shoddy goods, whereas those with plenty of money should make such a terrible fuss if there were the slightest fault in their purchases.

'What the hell d'you mean, North, by sending up this rubbish?' old Colonel Enderby had roared, flinging a pair of heavy gate hinges on to the counter, with such force that they skidded across, and would have crashed into young Bertie's chin if he had not ducked smartly. 'They're scratched!'

His father's politeness, in the face of this sort of behaviour, brought home to his son the necessity for knowing one's place on the social ladder. But it did not blind the child to a certain unfairness in his world's structure.

Standing at the high window, his bare feet growing more and more chilly on the cold linoleum, a new thought struck Bertie, as he watched Jim and Leslie far below. Were the Howards poor? They certainly had plenty to eat, delicious pies, new crusty loaves, and cakes in plenty; but they had very few toys, and Bertie's mother often gave Mrs Howard clothes, which Winnie had outgrown, for Kathy.

He remembered too, with some shock, that Jim's and Leslie's grandmother was old Mrs Bryant, the gipsy, who sometimes came into the shop, bent under her dirty black shawl. She certainly was poor. She spoke in a whining nasal voice and Bertie had heard her ask his father to take less than the marked price.

Did this mean that the Howard boys were on a par with the marsh children? His mother certainly spoke with some condescension about the Howards, Bertie recalled, but he knew very well that he would not be allowed to play with the marsh folk. Obviously then, the Howards were acceptable as play fellows.

It was all very puzzling, thought Bertie, resting his forehead against the cold glass. As far as he was concerned, Jim and Leslie were friends, even heroes, for when one is only eight one looks up to those of ten and twelve, especially when they are gracious enough to accept one's homage.

Through the window-pane, now misted with his breath,

Bertie saw Mrs Howard appear at the shop door and beckon her sons inside. Reluctantly, with backward glances, they obeyed and Bertie watched them vanish indoors. The shop door closed with a bang.

'Now *they've* got to go to bed!' said Bertie with satisfaction. And with this comforting thought he bounded into his own and was asleep in five minutes.

4. *First Encounter*

THE king recovered, and the nation rejoiced. Now the Coronation would be on August the ninth. The decorations, so sadly taken down, were restored to their places, and Queen Victoria peered once more from beneath her ribbon umbrella. The bells of St Peter's rang out merrily, calling across the countryside to a hundred others pealing from tower or soaring spire, among the downs and water meadows around Caxley.

Septimus Howard was doubly thankful for the King's recovery. On the morning after Edna's visit to Bender's shop he had called there himself, pale with anxiety. Bender had ushered him into the shop-parlour and closed the door.

'Say nothing, Sep,' he said. 'I know how it is.'

'I've got to say something,' burst out poor Sep. 'I haven't had a wink all night. I stand to lose nigh on forty pounds with cancelled orders, I reckon, and I can't see my way clear to paying you back what I owe for many a week.'

He passed an agitated hand over his white face.

'Look here, Sep,' rumbled Bender, 'you've got nothing to worry about. I know my money's safe enough. It'll come back one day, and it don't matter to me just when. Your business is coming along a fair treat. These 'ere set-backs happen to us all – but you keep plodding on, boy.'

He smote the smaller man a heartening blow on the shoulder which made his teeth rattle. Sep managed to produce a wan smile.

'It's good of you, Bender,' he began, but was cut short.

'More to the point, Sep – have you got enough to tide you over? Do you want a mite more till this business is straightened out?'

Sep's pale face flushed. His eyes were unhappy. He looked through the glass partition between the parlour and the shop and gazed at the kettles and saucepans, dangling from the ceiling there, with unseeing eyes.

'I think so. I think so, Bender. I'll know more tomorrow, and I don't want to borrow from you if I can help it. You've been generous enough already.'

He rose from the horse-hair chair and made his way to the door.

'Must get back to the shop. Plenty to do over there. People want loaves even if they don't want Coronation cakes.'

He turned and put out a timid hand. Bender gripped it painfully and pumped his arm vigorously up and down.

'Don't let things get you down, Sep,' boomed Bender cheerfully. 'That shop o' yours will be a blooming gold mine before you know where you are. Keep at it, old chap!'

'I only hope you're right,' poor Sep had replied, hurrying back to his duties.

But by August the ninth, with Coronation orders renewed, Sep had recovered his losses and made a handsome profit besides. By the end of that month, when he settled down, with Edna beside him, to cast up his accounts, he found that for the first time he was out of debt. Bender's loan had been repaid, so that the shop, furnishings, bakehouse and machinery, were now entirely their own. It was a day of thankful celebration in the Howard household.

From that moment, it seemed, fortune began to smile upon Sep and his family. The wedding cake for Miss Frances Hurley had been a creation of exquisite fragility, much commented upon by other well-born matrons at the wedding with daughters in the marriage lists. Sep's handiwork, and his competitive prices, were noted, and many an order came his way. Howard's bakery was beginning to earn the fine reputation it deserved. Sep himself could hardly believe his luck. Edna, excited by more money, needed restraining from gay and frivolous expenditure.

'Don't fritter it away,' begged poor Sep, bewildered but still prudent. ' 'Tis wrong, Edna, to be too free. There'll be plenty more rainy days to face. One swallow don't make a summer.'

With these and other cautious warnings Sep did his best to cool Edna's excitement. His strong chapel-guided principles deplored show and waste. Thrift, modesty, and humble bearing were ingrained in the little baker. He thanked his Maker for blessings received, but was too apprehensive to expect them to continue indefinitely. Nevertheless, a tidy sum began to accumulate steadily in the bank, the Howard boys had a new bicycle apiece, Edna glowed from beneath a pink hat, nodding with silk roses, as the Howards, as well as the Norths, began to share in the genial prosperity of Edward's golden reign.

It was a perfect time to be young. As the serene years slipped by, as slow and shining as the peaceful river Cax, the young Howards and Norths enjoyed all the wholesome pleasures of a small and thriving community. There was always something going on at the Corn Exchange, for this was the era of endless good works 'in aid of the poor' who were, alas, as numerous as ever. Concerts, plays, tableaux vivants, dances, socials, whist drives, and even roller-skating, followed each other in quick succession. The talent was local, the organization was local, and the appreciative audiences and participants were local too. There was something particularly warming in this family atmosphere. It had its stresses and strains, as all family relationships have, but the fact that each was known to the other, the virtues, the vices, the oddities and quirks of each individual were under common scrutiny, made for interest and amusement and bound the community at large with ties of affection and tolerance.

Bertie North now attended the town's grammar school daily and Winnie was one of the first pupils at the new girls' county school. Neither was outstandingly academic, but they were reasonably intelligent, obedient, and hard-working, and became deeply attached to their local schools, an affection which was to last a lifetime.

Despite the modest fees asked by these two establishments, and the diverse backgrounds of the pupils there, Sep could not bring himself to send his children to either, and they walked daily to the same National School in the High Street where he and Bender had been educated. The schooling was sound and the discipline strict. Bender, knowing something of Sep's finances, often argued with him to send his children elsewhere, but Sep was unwontedly stubborn on this point.

'The old school was good enough for me, Bender,' he replied. 'It'll do for my boys. No need for them to get ideas above their place.' And no amount of argument could budge him.

The children did not worry their heads about such distinctions. Life was much too full and fascinating. Every Thursday the market square's usual hum rose to a crescendo of shouting and clattering as the weekly market took place. The North and Howard children loved Thursdays. The day began very early, for long before breakfast time at seven o'clock the rumble of carts and the clop of horses' hooves woke the square. By the time the children set off for school everything was in full swing. Prudent town shoppers had already filled their baskets with fresh fruit and greens from the surrounding countryside before the country dwellers themselves arrived by trap or carrier cart to fill their own baskets with more sophisticated things. Everywhere was the sound of hooves and the sweet-sharp smell of horses.

For this was the golden age of the horse. Family coaches, some with fine crests on the doors, still rumbled through

Caxley from London to the west. Glossy carriages, with equally glossy high-steppers, bore the local gentry from one tea-party to another. Broughams and landaus, gigs and phaetons, traps and governess carts tapped and stuttered, rattled and reeled, round the square and onward. In the dusty country lanes, massive hay carts and wagons piled high with sacks or sheaves, swayed like galleons, with slow majesty, behind the teams of great cart horses, shaggy of hoof and mild of eye. The music of the horse and carriage was everywhere, the thunder of wheels and hoofs acting as bass to the treble of cracked whip and jingling harness. And always, as added accompaniment, there was the cry of man to horse, the encouraging chirrup, the staccato command, the endearment, with the appreciative snort or excited whinny in reply. It was an age when the horse was king, and his stabling, fodder, and well-being were paramount. He provided transport and labour, and the calm bright world was geared to his pace. The animal kingdom from man himself, who harnessed that willing and beautiful energy, down to the lowliest sparrow which fed upon his droppings, acknowledged the horse as peer. The thought that the smelly and new-fangled motor-car might one day supersede the horse never entered the heads of ordinary folk. Wasn't it true that London made the carriages, and England supplied the horses, for all the world? Nothing could alter that invincible fact.

It was the horse, in all its infinite variety, that the three boys chiefly encountered on their bicycle rides. Within five minutes of leaving the throbbing market place, they could be in the leafy lanes that led north, south, east and west from Caxley. The wide fields were fragrant with cut hay or bean flowers, freshly ploughed earth or ripe corn according to the season. The hedges were snowy with blossom or beaded with shiny berries. Blackbirds darted across their path. Speckled thrushes sang their hearts out from sprays of pear blossom in cottage gardens. There were butterflies of every hue fluttering on the flowered verges of the roadside, and when the boys rested in the cool grass under the shade of a hedge, they could hear all around them the tiny quiet noises of the countryside. Somewhere, high above, a lark carolled. In the dark thickness of the hedge a mouse scuffled the dry leaves stealthily. A bee bumbled lazily at the orange lips of toadflax flowers, and little winged insects hummed in the sunlight. These were the long happy hours of childhood which the boys were never to forget. The gentle countryside and its quiet villages were theirs to explore, and Caxley, small and secure, the beginning and the end of every adventure. Nothing, it seemed, could ruffle Caxley's age-old order.

But something did. In the midst of this halcyon period an event occurred which was to have far-reaching consequences. It began innocently enough, as such things so often do. It began with Dan Crockford's sudden hunger for one of Sep Howard's lardy cakes.

Daniel Crockford had lived in Caxley all his life, as had generations of Crockfords before him. The family had supplied woollen cloth to the town, and to all England – and parts of Europe for that matter – from the time when Caxley, in the sixteenth century, was building its prosperity from this industry. The family still owned a mill, but now it was a flour mill, some half-mile along the bank of the Cax from the market square.

Crockfords had played their part in the town's history and were well-liked. They had been Mayors, churchwardens, sidesmen, councillors, magistrates, and generous benefactors to many causes. But not one of them, until Dan appeared, had ever had anything to do with the arts. It would be true to say that the world of the imagination was looked upon with considerable suspicion and complete lack of interest by the worthy Crockfords.

It was all the more shocking, therefore, when the adolescent Daniel proclaimed that he intended to be an artist. His father was impatient, his mother tearful. What would the neighbours say?

'They'll say you're plain stark mad,' announced his father flatly. 'The mill needs you. There's a living waiting for you. If you must paint, then have the common sense to do it in your spare time!'

'They'll say you're no better than you should be,' wailed his mother. 'You know how wild and shameless artists are! It's common knowledge! Oh, the disgrace to us all!'

The young man remained unmoved. A few uncomfortable months passed and at last his father paid for him to go to an art school in London for two years.

'Let him work it out of his system,' he growled to his wife. But Dan throve on the work, his reports were reassuring and he returned to his home determined to make painting his career. His father, seeing that the boy's mind was made up, had a studio built at the back of the house in Caxley, and let him have his way. There were other sons to take an interest in the mill, and Dan had a small income from an indulgent uncle and godfather which covered his essential needs. The Crockford family was resigned to the black sheep among the rest of the flock.

Dan sold an occasional landscape to various local people who had wall space to fill. His views of the Cax were considered very pretty and life-like. His portraits were thought unflattering, and rather too garish in colour. With photography becoming so cheap and reliable it seemed sinful to spend so much money on having a portrait painted which might not please when it was done.

But Dan worked away happily, and did not appear to mind that the stacks of paintings grew in his studio and very seldom sold. He was a large handsome man of flamboyant appearance, with a wealth of red hair and a curling red beard. He loved food, and he loved drink even more. Tales of Dan Crockford's prowess in the bars of Caxley and the country inns near by grew tall in the telling. He wore a dark wide-brimmed hat and big floppy silk ties. He had taken up the work of an artist, and he intended to make it plain. Needless to say, he was looked upon in Caxley as a somewhat worthless character, and his family, everyone said, was to be pitied.

On this particular morning, Dan had spent over an hour in cleaning his brushes and his nostrils were filled with the reek of turpentine. It was a soft May morning and the door of the studio was propped open with an old velvet-covered chair. On it, asleep in the sunshine, the family tabby cat rested a chin on its outstretched paws.

The turpentine had run out, and intrigued with the texture and markings of the cat's leonine head, Dan took a piece of charcoal and began to sketch intently. He brushed in the soft ruff, the upward sweep of grey whiskers and the fluff protruding from the pricked black ears. Delicately he sketched in the intricate frown marks of the forehead, the rows of black dots from which sprang whiskers on the upper part of the muzzle, and the bars which ran, echelon fashion, along each jaw.

He began to feel excitement rising. The sketch was good. He selected a firmer piece of charcoal and began the difficult job of emphasising the streak of each closed eye and the puckering of the mouth.

Suddenly, the cat woke, yawned, leapt down, and vanished. Furious, Dan swore, flung away the charcoal and burst from the studio into the garden. He found that he was shaking with fury. He would take a brief walk to calm himself. He picked up the empty turpentine bottle, resolved to get it filled at North's, have a quick drink and return to work.

Swinging the bottle, his great hat crammed on the back of

his red head, he strode through the market place. There were several people outside the baker's shop and he was forced to step close to the window in order to pass them. A wave of spicy fragrance floated from the open door. Sep was putting a trayful of sticky brown lardy cakes in the window, and Dan realized that he was desperately hungry. He stepped down into the shop, and saw, for the first time, Edna Howard.

It was a shock as sudden and delightful as a plunge into the Cax on a hot afternoon. Dan knew beauty, when he saw it, by instinct and by training. This was the real thing, warm, gracious, dynamic. In one intent glance he noted the dark soft wings of hair, the upward sweep of the cheekbones, the angle of the small pink ears, and the most beautiful liquid brown eyes he had ever seen. Dan gazed in amazement. To think that this beauty had remained hidden from him so long!

'Sir?' asked Sep deferentially.

Dan wrenched his eyes away.

'Oh, ah!' he faltered. He fumbled in his pocket for a sixpence. 'One of your lardy cakes, if you please.'

While Sep busied himself in wrapping up his purchase in fine white paper, Dan looked again. Edna had walked across the shop to a shelf where she was stacking loaves. Her figure was as exquisite as her face, her movements supple. There was something oddly foreign about her which excited Dan.

He found Sep holding out the bag. He was looking at him curiously.

'Thanks. Good day to you,' said Dan briskly, and departed towards the river bank.

There, sitting on the grassy bank beneath a may tree, he devoured his fresh, warm lardy cake and made plans.

She must sit for him. He must go back again and ask her. She was the perfect subject for his type of portrait – full of colour, warmth, and movement. She must be Sep Howard's wife. He groped in his memory.

Of course! What had the old wives said? 'He married beneath him – a *Bryant*, you know!'

Dan leapt to his feet, and banged the crumbs from his clothes.

'"The gipsy",' he cried. 'That's what we'll call it: "The Gipsy Girl"!'

5. *Domestic Rebellion*

DAN fought down the impulse to return at once to Sep's shop and hurried home instead. By judicious questioning of his mother, he confirmed that the beautiful girl was indeed Sep Howard's wife.

In his studio, he wrote a brief note to say that he would give himself the pleasure of calling upon Mr and Mrs Howard that evening at eight o'clock, on a matter of business, and dispatched it by the little maid-of-all-work. The hours until that time seemed excessively tedious to the impatient artist.

'I can't think why he didn't say anything in the shop this morning,' said Sep, much puzzled, as he read the note.

'Maybe it's only just come to his mind,' suggested Edna, busy mending baby clothes and not much interested in the letter.

'Seems funny to address it to *both* of us,' went on Sep. Dan Crockford's open admiration of his wife had not escaped Sep's sensitive eye.

'He probably only wants you to do a bit of catering for a party or something,' said Edna off-handedly. She snapped the cotton with her white teeth, and folded up the baby's gown.

Prompt at eight, Dan arrived. Edna and Sep received him in the first floor parlour which was at the back of the house overlooking the yard and the distant Cax. The willows lining the banks were shimmering green and gold in their new May finery, and Edna wore a dress which matched their colour. In her presence Dan felt strangely shy, as he was introduced. Sep, who had known the Crockfords slightly for many years, was obviously ill at ease. Edna was quite unperturbed.

'I believe you want to discuss business matters,' she said, rising. 'I'll be with the children if you need me.'

Dan leapt to his feet in alarm.

'Don't go! Please, Mrs Howard, don't go! The business concerns you too, I assure you.'

Wonderingly, Edna slowly resumed her seat. Dan, still standing, wasted no more time but swiftly outlined his proposal. It would be doing him a great honour. He realized that she was very busy. Any time which would suit her convenience would suit his too. It was usual to pay sitters, and he hoped that she would name her fee. He would try to do justice to her outstanding good looks.

The words tumbled out in a vast torrent now that he had begun. Edna gazed upon him in amazement, her beautiful eyes wide and wondering. Sep grew paler as the scheme was unfolded. What impudence, what idiocy, was this?

At last Dan came to a halt, and Edna spoke shyly.

'It's very kind of you, I'm sure. I don't quite know what to think.' She looked at Sep in perplexity. Clearly, she was a little flattered, and inclined to consider the project.

Sep found his voice.

'We'll have nothing to do with it,' he said hoarsely. 'I'm not having my wife mixed up in things of this sort. We don't want the money, thank God, and my wife wouldn't want to earn it that way, I can assure you. I mean no offence, Mr Crockford. Your affairs are your own business, and good luck to your painting. But don't expect Edna to take part.'

Dan was frankly taken aback by the force of the meek little baker's attack. The thought that there would be such fierce opposition had not entered his mind. He spoke gently, controlling his temper, fearing that Edna would be surely lost to him as a sitter, if it flared up now.

'Don't close your mind to the idea, please,' he begged. 'Think about it and talk the matter over with your wife, and let me know in a few days. I fear that I have taken you too much by surprise. I very much trust that you will allow me to paint Mrs Howard. She would not need to sit for more than three or four sessions.'

Calmer, but still seething inwardly, Sep acknowledged the wisdom of discussing the matter. His old timidity towards those in the social class above him began to make itself felt again. One could not afford to offend good customers, and although his face was firmly set against Edna's acceptance, he deemed it wise to bring the interview to an outwardly civil close.

He accompanied Dan to the door and showed him out into the market square.

'We will let you know,' he said shortly, 'though I must make it plain that I don't like the idea, and very much doubt if Edna will agree.'

He watched Dan swing across the square on his homeward way. His red hair flamed in the dying sun's rays. His chin was at a defiant angle. Dan Crockford was a handsome man, thought Sep sadly, and a fighting man too.

Suddenly weary, conscious that he must return to face Edna, he caught sight of Queen Victoria, proudly defiant, despite a pigeon poised absurdly on her bronze crown.

'And what would she have thought of it?' wondered Sep morosely, turning his back on the market place.

The scene that ensued was never to be forgotten by poor Sep.

'Well, that's seen the back of that cheeky rascal!' announced Sep, on returning to the parlour. He assumed a brisk authority which he did not feel inwardly, but he intended to appear as master in his own house.

'Who says we've seen the back of him?' asked Edna, dangerously calm.

'I do. I've sent him about his business all right.'

'It was my business, too, if you remember. Strikes me you jumped in a bit sharp. Never gave me time to think it over, did you?'

'I should hope a respectable married woman like you would need no time at all to refuse that sort of invitation.' Sep spoke with a certain pomposity which brought Edna to her feet. She leant upon the table, eyes flashing, and faced her husband squarely.

'You don't appear to trust me very far, Sep Howard. I ain't proposing to stand stark naked for Mr Crockford –'

'I should hope not!' broke in Sep, much shocked.

'It was me he wanted to paint. And I should have had the chance of answering. Made me look no better than a stupid kid, snapping back at him like that, and leaving me out of things.'

Sep buttoned his mouth tightly. He had become very pale and the righteous wrath of generations of staunch chapel-goers began to make his blood boil.

'There's no more to be said, my lady. It was a shameful suggestion and I'll not see my wife flaunting herself for Dan Crockford or anyone else. I don't want to hear any more about it.'

If Sep had been in any condition to think coolly, he must have realized that this was the best way to rouse a mettlesome wife to open rebellion. But he was not capable of thinking far ahead just then. He watched the colour flood Edna's lovely face and her thin brown hands knot into tight fists.

'You don't want to hear any more about it, eh?' echoed Edna. Her voice was low, and throbbing with fury. 'Well, let me tell you, Sep Howard, you're going to! I should like to have my picture painted. Dan Crockford don't mean anything more to me than that chair there, but if he wants to paint my picture, I'm willing. You can't stop me, and you'd better not try, unless you wants to run the shop, and the home too, on your own. I won't be bossed about by you, or anyone else!'

It was at this dangerous moment in the battle that Sep should have given in completely, apologized for his arrogance, told Edna that he could not do without her, and that of course she could sit for Dan Crockford if she wanted to so desperately. Edna's defiance would have abated at once, and all would have been forgotten. But Sep made the wrong move. He thumped the table and shouted.

'I forbid –' he began in a great roaring voice which stirred the curtains.

'Forbid?' screamed Edna. 'Don't you take that tone to me, you little worm! Who d'you think you're talking to – our Kathy? I'm going up to bed now, and tomorrow morning I'm going round to Dan Crockford's to tell him I'll sit for him!'

She whirled from the room, her gold and green dress swishing, leaving Sep open-mouthed. Here was flat rebellion, and Sep knew full well that he had no weapon in his armoury to overcome it.

Morning brought no truce, and Edna set out purposefully across the square as soon as her house was set to rights. Sep watched her go, dumb with misery.

By the time market day came round again the whole of Caxley buzzed with this delicious piece of news. Fat Mrs Petty, chopping cod into cutlets, shouted boisterously above the rhythmic noise of her cleaver.

'No better'n she should be! Once a gyppo, always a gyppo, I says! And us all knows what Dan Crockford's like.'

'It's her poor husband I feel so sorry for,' nodded her customer lugubriously. Her mouth was set in a deprecating downward curve, but her eyes were gleaming with enjoyment. Gossip is always interesting, and this was a particularly exciting snippet for the good folk of Caxley.

'It won't surprise me to hear that Sep Howard turns her out,' continued the customer with relish. 'Been brought up proper strict, his lot – chapel every Sunday, Band of Hope, and all that. You never know, it might all end up in the court!'

She looked across at Caxley's Town Hall, standing beside St Peter's. Two magistrates were already mounting the steps, dignified in their good broadcloth, for the weekly sitting. Mrs Petty broke into loud laughter, holding up two fat hands, sparkling with fish-scales.

'Court?' she wheezed merrily. 'Ain't no need to take Edna Howard to court! All her husband needs is to take a strap to her!'

In this, Mrs Petty echoed most people in Caxley. If Sep's wife behaved like this, they said, then Sep was at fault. He knew what he'd taken on when he married her. He should have been firm.

The Norths watched the affair closely, and with dismay. Bender was inclined to dismiss it as 'a storm in a tea-cup'. Edna would come to her senses in time. But Hilda felt some inner triumph. Hadn't she always said that Edna wasn't to be trusted?

'One thing,' she admitted, 'it's bringing our Ethel round to seeing the truth about Dan Crockford. Pa said she was quite cool with him when they met in the street. And Jesse Miller's no fool. He's been up at Pa's every evening this week, hanging up his hat to our Ethel.'

'It don't do to make bad blood anywhere,' rumbled Bender, 'especially in a little place like Caxley. We've all got to rub along together, come fair, come foul, and the sooner this business blows over the better. No need to fan the flames now, Hilda.'

His wife bridled, but said no more.

But the flames ran everywhere, fanned smartly by the wind of gossip. That this should have happened to meek little Septimus Howard, strict chapel-goer, diligent baker, and earnest father, made the affair even more delectable. It was said that Edna went twice a week to Dan's studio, unchaperoned, in the evening, and that no one could really tell what happened there, although, of course, it was easy enough to guess.

Even the children heard the tales, and young Bertie asked the two Howard boys if their mother really had let Mr Crockford paint her picture. To his everlasting horror, one boy burst into tears and the other gave him such a swinging box on the ear that he fell into the thorn bush and was obliged to lie to his mother later about how he had become so severely scratched. Certainly, Edna's portrait created enough stir.

In actual fact the sittings were few and rather dull. They did occur, as rumour said, twice weekly and in the evening, but after six sessions Dan assured his model that he could finish it without troubling her further. Her beauty delighted him, but her dullness bored him dreadfully. Her independence having been proved, Edna was quite willing to make things up with her unhappy husband, and outwardly at least, harmony once again prevailed in the Howards' household.

But the matter did not end there.

The picture was enchanting. Dan knew in his bones that this was the best piece of work he had ever done. Edna glowed from the canvas, gay and vivid, in her gipsy costume. She made a compelling figure, for Dan had caught her warmth and grace magnificently. Furthermore, he had painted a perfect woodland background in minute detail. All the fresh haziness of a May morning sparkled behind Edna – a smoke-blue wood, with pigeons like pearls sunning themselves in the branches, above a grassy bank, starred with daisies, and almost golden in its May newness. He had caught exactly the spirit of wild young life in all its glory. Dan put it aside carefully to be sent to the Academy early next year. This one, surely, would find a place on those august walls.

Meantime, while the gossip ran rife, Howard's bakery suffered a temporary decline. A few self-righteous families refused to deal with a baker whose wife behaved so loosely. Others were embarrassed at facing Sep and preferred to slip into other bakers' establishments until the family affairs were righted. It was an unfortunate set-back for poor Sep who felt his position keenly. There were times when he longed to shut up the shop and flee from Caxley, from the sidelong glances, the whispers behind hands, the wretched knowledge that all knew his discomfiture.

He had said little to Edna after that first terrible encounter. There was so little to say which did not sound nagging, pompous, and bitter. Sep told himself that 'the least said soonest mended' and continued doggedly with his business affairs. Apart from a certain coolness, Edna continued her household duties unconcerned. When the sittings came to an end, tension between the two relaxed slightly, but, for Sep at least, things could never be quite the same again.

In time, of course, Caxley began to lose interest in the affair as other topics took the place of the portrait painting as a nine days' wonder. The scandal of the erring alderman, the bankruptcy of an old family business, the elopement of a local farmer's son with a pretty dairymaid, and many other delightful pieces of news came to the sharp eyes and ears of Caxley folk and engaged their earnest attention. It was not until the following year that the Howard scandal was suddenly revived and bathed now in miraculous sunlight instead of shadow.

For Dan Crockford's picture was accepted by the Hanging Committee of the Royal Academy and was one of the paintings of the year. *The Caxley Chronicle* printed this wonderful news on the front page, with a photograph of Dan Crockford and another of the portrait. The headline read: 'Well Deserved Success for Distinguished Local Artist', and the account mentioned 'the beauty of Mrs Septimus Howard, captured for posterity by the skill of the artist's brush.'

This put quite a different complexion on the affair, of course. If *The Caxley Chronicle* thought Dan Crockford was distinguished, then the majority of its readers were willing to believe it. And say what you like, they told each other reasonably, when they met the following week, he'd made a proper handsome picture of Sep's wife and it was a real leg-up for Caxley all round.

People now called at the bakery to see the celebrated Mrs Howard, and poor bewildered Sep found himself accepting congratulations in place of guarded condolences. It was a funny world, thought Sep, that kicked you when you were down, and patted you when you were up again, and all for the same reason.

Nevertheless, it was pleasant to find that the takings had risen sharply since the news came out. And he readily admitted that it was pleasanter still to be greeted warmly, by all and sundry, as he carried his hard-earned money across the market square to the bank. Pray God, thought Sep earnestly, things would now go smoothly for them all!

6. *Local Election*

THINGS went very smoothly indeed in the early part of the century. Trade was brisk generally, and despite the high new motor-cars which began to sail majestically down Caxley High Street like galleons before the wind, though with somewhat more noise, the stablemen, coachmen, farriers, and the multitude of men engaged in ministering to the horse, still thrived.

It was true that Bill Blake's cycle shop at the marsh end of the High Street had begun repairing cars, and had taken over a yard at the side of the premises for this purpose. Under the shade of a vast sycamore tree against the rosy brick wall, Bill and his brother investigated the complicated interiors of the newcomers, surrounded by the enthusiastic small fry of Caxley. But the idea of the motor car ever superseding the ubiquitous horse was never really considered seriously by those who watched with such absorption.

The Howard boys had been among the keenest students of the early motor car, and as they grew older did their best to persuade Sep to discard the two horse-drawn vans, which now took his expanding business further afield, and to buy a motorvan. But Sep would have none of it. It would cost too much. It would break down. He preferred his horses.

By the time King Edward died in 1910 and his son George was made King, both boys were in the bakery business. Jim was now twenty-one and Leslie nineteen. Jim was like his father in looks and temperament, neat, quiet, and industrious. His presence in the shop was invaluable, and as Sep grew older, he was glad to give more responsibility to his first-born.

Leslie took after Edna, dark, volatile, and with the same devastating good looks. To be seen dancing the polka with Leslie at the Corn Exchange was something the girls of Caxley thoroughly enjoyed.

It was Leslie who bowled round the country lanes in the baker's van, touching his cap politely to the gentry as he edged Dandy the mare into the hedgerow to let a carriage – and sometimes a brand-new tonneau – pass by. It was Leslie who won the hearts of the old country women with his cheerful quips as he went on his rounds.

'A real nice lad,' they would say to each other, a warm loaf held in the crook of their arms as they watched Leslie and the mare vanish in a cloud of dust. 'Got his ma's looks, ain't he? But takes after his pa, too, let's hope.'

The growth of Sep's fortunes had brought him into the public eye. He had been persuaded to stand as a candidate in the local elections, and, much to his surprise, was successful in gaining a seat on the council. Caxley recognized the integrity and strength of character which was hidden behind his diffident appearance. His family and his business flourished, and his conduct over the portrait affair, which had been so severely criticized at the time, was now spoken of with praise.

'Sets a real example to that family of his! Look how forbearing he was with his Edna! Some would've kicked her out of doors, behaving that way. But you see, it's all turned out for the best, and she've quietened down into a thorough good wife.'

Edna certainly gained dignity as the years passed. She still sang in public, and still played her banjo in private. But memories are long in the country, and Edna was still looked upon with some suspicion by the good ladies who organized charity events. Not so Hilda North, whose help was asked for on many occasions. It gave Hilda much private satisfaction to be invited to serve on committees with the local gentry, particularly as Edna was never so invited. Their children remained firm friends, and their husbands too, but the two wives grew cooler with each other as the years passed.

Hilda, in the early days of the new reign, now had three children. Bertie was seventeen and intended going into the motor trade, Winifred fifteen, still at the High School and longing to finish there and start training as a nurse. It was on Winnie's twelfth birthday that Hilda had discovered that she was having another child – an event which she greeted with mingled dismay and pleasure, for she had thought her family complete and was looking forward to an end to cots and prams and all the paraphernalia of babyhood. But Bender was whole-heartedly delighted with the news.

'Always the best – those that aren't ordered,' he assured his wife. 'You mark my words, she'll be a beauty.'

Amazingly enough, it was indeed a girl, and a beauty. At four she was as pretty as a picture with fair curls and eyes as blue as speedwell flowers. She was also thoroughly spoilt by all the family and hair-raisingly outspoken.

When Lady Hurley called to enlist Hilda's aid in raising money for a Christmas fund for the poor of Caxley, the tea table had been laden with the best china, the silver teapot and wafer-thin bread and butter. The lightest of sponge cakes crowned a silver dish, and three sorts of jam, flanked by Gentlemen's Relish, added distinction to the scene.

While Hilda was plying her honoured guest, young Mary put her head round the door and interrupted the genteel conversation.

'Our cat sicked up just before you came,' she volunteered in a clear treble voice. 'He sicked up half a mouse and a –'

'That'll do!' said poor Hilda hastily. She rang the bell and Mary was removed, protesting loudly, to the kitchen. It was a scene which the family remembered with pleasure for years, and Hilda with the deepest mortification.

Hilda's sense of propriety was strongly developed. She enjoyed her position in Caxley society and was proud to be the wife of a well-to-do tradesman, churchwarden, and well-known public figure. She liked to be seen entering St Peter's for Matins, clad in her best gown and mantle in suitably quiet colours, dove-grey perhaps, or deep mauve, with a sedate hat to match, trimmed with pansies or a wide watered-silk ribbon. She retained her trim figure over the years, and tight lacing contributed to her neat appearance.

She was proud too of her family, good-looking and robust, even if not over-blessed with brains. Winifred, now growing up fast, would never be the beauty that little Mary promised to be, but she had a fresh fairness which the boys seemed to find attractive. Somewhat to Hilda's annoyance, she suspected that Leslie Howard, old enough to have chosen someone among his numerous admirers for his particular choice, cast a roving eye upon his friend of a life-time. An alliance with the Howard family was not to be borne. Winifred was to do much better for herself. Climbing the social ladder was an exercise which Hilda accomplished with ease and dexterity. There was no reason on earth why a girl like Winifred should not marry happily into the gentry, if the cards were played with discretion.

As for Bertie, Hilda's heart melted whenever her eye rested upon him. He had always been particularly dear, perhaps because he followed so soon upon the stillborn son who was their first child, and gave them so much comfort when it was sorely needed. At eighteen Bertie was as tall as his massive father, but long-limbed and slender. His fair hair had not darkened much with the years, and his quiet grave good looks were much admired.

There was a reserve about Bertie which set him a little apart from the rest of the Norths. Always cheerful in company, he also loved solitude. He liked to dawdle by the Cax, or hang over the bridge, watching the smooth water glide below, whispering through the reeds at the bank side and weaving ever-changing patterns across the river bed. Perhaps he had noise enough at his work at Blake's, for he had just started a course of motor engineering with that firm. It was work that absorbed him. He had patience and physical strength, and a ready grasp of mechanics. He was certain, too, in his own mind, that the motor-car had come to stay despite the scoffings of his elders. Above all, he was secretly thankful that he was not in the family business, for Bender's somewhat slap-dash methods irked him, and he was too respectful a son to criticize his father.

On the face of it, the business flourished. The Norths now owned their own horse and trap, for Uncle Ted's little cob had been sold when the old man grew too frail for driving, and it was now Bender's turn to take his elder brother on an occasional visit in the family trap. A freshly-painted skiff was moored at the end of the Norths' small garden, and once every year the shop was left in charge of Bob, now second-in-command, still with a mop of unruly black hair and steel spectacles set awry, while the family took a week's holiday at the sea. Caxley never doubted that Bender's business was as flourishing as ever.

But Bender himself knew otherwise. His turnover had not increased in the past few years, and now there was a serious threat to the business. The great firm of Tenby's, which flourished in the county town, opened a branch next door to Blake's at the marsh end of Caxley High Street. Their premises were far grander and far larger than Bender's, and the new agricultural machinery, which was beginning to make its way on to the market, was displayed and demonstrated with great ease in the commodious covered yard behind the shop.

It was Jesse Miller who brought the seriousness of the

position home to Bender. He was a frequent caller now at the Norths', for he had succeeded in persuading the vacillating Ethel, Hilda North's sister, to marry him a few years earlier when Dan Crockford's behaviour appeared so reprehensible to the sterner eyes of Caxley.

The two men sat smoking in the snug murk of the shop parlour one November evening. Outside the pavements were wet with the clinging fog which wreathed its way from the Cax valley to twine itself about the gas lamps of the market place.

Above their heads the gas hissed, and a bright fire flickered cheerfully in the little round-arched grate.

'Got a good fire there,' observed Jesse, watching Bender's ministrations with the steel poker.

'Coal's cheap enough,' answered Bender, widening a crack with a smart blow. 'Can still afford that, thank God!'

Jesse Miller blew a long blue cloud towards the ceiling. He watched it disperse reflectively and then took a deep breath.

'Look, Bender! I've had something on my mind for some time and I reckon it's best to speak out. Am I right in thinking the shop's not paying its way?'

Bender's face flushed and the deep colour flooded his bull neck, but he answered equably.

'I'd not go that far, Jesse. We're not bankrupt yet, if that's what's on your mind.'

'But it's not as good as it was?' persisted Jesse, leaning forward.

'Well, no,' admitted Bender, with a sigh. He thrust out his long legs and the horse-hair chair creaked a protest. 'Bound to be a bit of a drop in takings when a shop like Tenby's first opens. People like to bob in and see what's there. They'll come back, I don't doubt.'

'I do,' said Jesse forcefully. 'You might as well face it –

Tenby's are here for good, and they'll offer more than you ever can.'

Bender was about to protest, but Jesse Miller waved him aside.

'It's not only the room they've got; they've got keen chaps too. And another thing, they're quick with getting the stuff to the customer. I've had a couple of harrows on order here since Michaelmas, and where are they?'

'You know dam' well where they are,' rumbled Bender, beginning to look surly. 'Down in Wiltshire where they're made, and where they're too idle to put 'em on the railway! I've written to them time and time again!'

'Maybe! It don't alter the fact, Bender, that Tenby's have got a dozen stacked in their yard now, and if you can't get mine here by next week – I'm telling you straight, man – I'm going there for a couple.'

The two men glared at each other, breathing heavily. They were both fighters, and both obdurate.

'Oh, you are, are you?' growled Bender. 'Well, I daresay the old business can manage without your custom for once, though I think it's a pretty mean sort of thing for one friend to do to another.'

Jesse relaxed, and tapped his pipe out on the bars of the grate.

'See here,' he said in a softer tone, as he straightened up, 'I'm not the only chap in these parts who's feeling the same way. If you want to keep your customers you'll darn well have to put yourself out a bit more, Bender. You're too easy-going by half, and Tenby's are going to profit by it.'

'Maybe, maybe!' agreed Bender.

'And what's all this I hear about you putting up for the council? Can you spare the time?'

'That's my business. I was asked to stand, and Hilda agrees it's a good thing.'

'Against Sep Howard? He's had a good majority each time.'

'Why not against Sep Howard? We know each other well enough to play fair. Sep's quite happy about it, that I do know.'

Jesse Miller sighed, and pocketed his pipe.

'Well, Bender, you know what you're doing, I suppose, but if this business were mine, I wouldn't waste my time and energy on anything else but putting it back on its feet again.'

He rose to his feet and lifted his greatcoat from the hook on the door.

'What does young Bertie think about it all?' he asked, shrugging himself into the coat.

'He knows nothing about it,' replied Bender shortly. 'I'm not panicking simply because the takings are down a bit on last year. The business will be as good as ever when it's time for me to hand it over.'

'I wonder!' commented Jesse Miller, and vanished round the door.

Bender had cause to remember this conversation in the months that followed. Trade began to wane to such an extent that it was quite clear that many people, particularly farmers, were transferring their custom to Tenby's and would continue to do so. It was not in Bender's nature to be alarmed, but he went about his business very much more soberly.

The local election did much to distract his mind from the depressing state of affairs. The third contestant was a local schoolteacher of advanced ideas, with a fine flow of rhetoric when unchecked, but having no ability to stand up to bucolic hecklers. Sep and Bender agreed that he would constitute no great menace to either of them.

When Sep had first heard that Bender was opposing him,

he felt the old sick fluttering in his stomach which had afflicted him in Bender's presence ever since his schooldays. It was absurd, he told himself for the hundredth time, to let the man affect him in this way. Sep was now a man of some substance, although his way of life had changed little. He attended chapel as regularly as ever, accompanied by Edna and the family. Sometimes, it is true, Leslie was not present, but when you are twenty, and as attractive as Leslie Howard, it was not to be wondered at, the more indulgent matrons of Caxley told each other.

Sep had been a councillor now for several years. He looked upon this present fight as a private challenge – not between Bender and himself – but to his own courage. In chapel, his head sunk upon his hands, Sep prayed earnestly and silently for help in overcoming his own fears. He did not pray that he might win – it would have been as despicable as it was presumptuous to do so; but he prayed that he might fight the fight bravely and honourably.

There was no doubt about it, Bender was going to be a formidable opponent. He was well-liked, he had a commanding presence, and a breezy sense of humour which stood him in good stead when the heckling began. Sep knew he could not compete with Bender in this field, but he could only hope that his record of steady service to the town would keep his supporters loyal.

The boys and girls of the two families thoroughly enjoyed the excitement. They cycled up and down the Caxley streets, stuffing pamphlets through letter-boxes and nailing up election posters on doors and railings. There was no hostility between the two parties, as far as the younger generation was concerned. Winifred North and Kathy Howard accompanied each other on these expeditions, and were not above taking one side of each road and posting both notices through the boxes, with superb magnanimity.

Sep and Bender approached their electioneering in typical

fashion. It was the custom to take turns in having the market place for an open-air meeting. Bender addressed the crowd in a hearty voice which could be heard clearly. His eyes sparkled, his arms waved in generous and compelling movements. Here was a man who enjoyed the publicity, the excitement, and the fight. His hearers warmed to him.

The evenings when Sep took the little platform, close by Queen Victoria, were much more sedate. Small, pale, his gentle voice scarcely audible, Sep nevertheless managed to command attention. There was a sincerity about him which appealed to his listeners, and moreover his past work was generally appreciated. It was hard to forecast which of the two men would win the election. Caxley seemed fairly equally divided in its loyalties.

On the great day, the schools were used as polling stations, much to the gratification of the local children. Bender and Sep, taking brief spells off from their businesses, ranged the town in their traps to take the infirm to register their votes. It happened to be market day in Caxley, and so the bustle was greater than ever.

By the time polling ended both men were tense and tired. Counting went on at the Town Hall next door to St Peter's. This edifice, built in the middle years of the old Queen's reign, was of a repellent fish-paste red, picked out, here and there, with a zig-zag motive in yellow tiles. It contrasted sadly with the mellow honey-coloured stone of the noble church beside it, but on this day its architectural shortcomings were ignored, for here, on the red brick balcony would be announced the name of the victorious candidate.

It was almost eleven o'clock when at last the Mayor and other officials made their entrance high above the square. The upturned faces grew suddenly still, and the noise of a distant train could be clearly heard chuffing its way rhythmically out of Caxley Station a mile away.

The three candidates stood self-consciously beside the scarlet-clad Mayor.

'John Emmanuel Abbott, two hundred and thirty-four,' read the Mayor sonorously. There was a mingled sound of cheering and booing. The little schoolteacher preserved a dignified and tight-lipped silence and bowed slightly.

'Septimus Howard, six thousand, nine hundred and two.' More cheers arose, hastily checked as the Mayor lifted his paper again.

'Bertram Lewis North, four thousand, seven hundred and twenty-two,' intoned the Mayor.

Now the cheering broke out anew, and when Septimus Howard, elected once more, stepped forward shyly, someone began to clap and shout: 'Good old Sep!' It was taken up by almost all the crowd, a spontaneous gesture of affection which was as touching as it was unexpected.

Sep bowed his thanks, spoke briefly of the honour done him, and promised to do his best to be worthy of the confidence shown in him. He turned to shake the hands of his opponents, first that of John Abbott, and then Bender's.

At that moment, their hands tightly clasped, Sep experienced a shock. Bender's smile was as broad as ever, his complexion as ruddy, but it was the expression in his eyes, the look of hurt wonderment, which shook Sep so profoundly. For the first time in his life, Sep felt pity for the great giant of a man before him, and, as well as pity, a new deep and abiding peace.

Amidst the tumult of the crowd and the dazzle of the lights, Sep became conscious of one outstanding truth. Within him, born suddenly of this strange new feeling, was an inner calm and strength. Somehow, Sep knew, it would remain there, and would colour his relationship towards Bender in the years ahead.

7. *Love Affairs*

LIKE many other bluff, hearty men who seem to ride boldly through life, Bender was easily upset. The outcome of the election was a considerable shock to him. That his fellow townsmen preferred Sep's services to his own was particularly humiliating. Not that Bender disparaged Sep's industry and sincerity, but he could not help feeling a certain condescending amusement at what he called 'Sep's bible-thumping' attitude to life. As a lifelong church-goer, Bender tended to underestimate the strength of Methodism in Caxley, and though this did not influence the outcome entirely, yet he could not help realizing that many chapel-goers had voted for Sep. His easy tolerance of nonconformists now suffered a change. Smarting secretly from his hurt, Bender was inclined to view the chapel-goers with a little more respect and, it must be admitted, with a twinge of sourness.

It was not surprising, therefore, that he was unusually waspish when Hilda told him of her fears about Leslie Howard and Winifred.

'I'm beginning to think,' Hilda said, 'that there's more to it than just being friendly. Our Winnie's at a silly age, let's face it, and Leslie's had plenty of practice turning young girls' heads.'

'Probably nothing in it,' replied Bender, pacifying womanly doubts automatically. 'But we certainly don't want our girl mixed up with the chapel lot.'

'It's not "being mixed up with the chapel lot", as you call it,' retorted Hilda, with unwonted spirit, 'but Leslie's been mixed up with too many girls already! Besides,' she continued, 'there are better fish in the sea for our Winnie than Sep Howard's boy.'

'You've no call to speak like that about Sep,' admonished Bender, secretly regretting his hasty disparagement of the Howards' religion.

'But surely you don't want anything to come of this?' demanded Hilda, putting down her crochet work as though about to do battle. Bender began to retreat. He had enough worries with the uncertainties of the business and the shock of the election without adding this problem to the list. He took a man's way out.

'You have a quiet word with Winnie, my dear. You'll handle it better than I can. And if I get a chance I'll just mention it to Sep and he can speak to Leslie. But ten chances to one, you're worrying yourself about nothing. Damn it all, Hilda, our Winnie's not nineteen!'

'I married you at that age,' pointed out Hilda tartly. She picked up her crochet work again, and stabbed sharply, in and out, with unusual ferocity.

As might be expected, Bender said nothing to Sep or anyone else about Leslie's attentions to his daughter. But Hilda approached her task with circumspection one evening when she and Winifred were alone in the kitchen. Her daughter blushed a becoming pink, twirled a tea-cloth rapidly round and round inside a jug, but said remarkably little.

Hilda, washing up busily at the sink, went a trifle further.

'Not that there's anything against the Howards, dear, or you would never have been allowed to be such good friends with the family, but it's as well to let it remain at that.'

'How d'you mean?' asked Winifred.

Really, thought Hilda, fishing exasperatedly for a teaspoon lurking in the depths, Winnie was sometimes very awkward!

'What I say! People are beginning to notice that you and Leslie dance a great deal together, and go for walks alone –

all that sort of thing – and naturally they wonder if they're going to hear of an engagement.'

'You'd hear first,' said Winnie briefly.

It was not the sort of answer which gave Hilda any comfort. She began to feel that she was not making much progress.

'So I would hope! It doesn't alter the fact that Leslie is paying you a great deal of attention. He's in his twenties now, and he'll be thinking of marriage before long. You're only eighteen.'

'You were married at nineteen,' pointed out the maddening girl. Hilda tipped out the washing-up water, advanced upon the towel on the back door, and sent the wooden roller rumbling thunderously as she dried her hands energetically. It seemed that the time had come for plain speaking.

'What I'm trying to make you see, Winnie, is that there are other young men in Caxley – and *better placed* young men – who would most certainly make you happier than Leslie Howard when the time comes. Just be warned, my dear, and don't get entangled before you've had a chance to look round you. Leslie's well known as a charmer, and you don't want to be left high and dry, as so many of the others have, when Leslie's lost interest.'

Winifred continued to polish the jug. Her eyes were downcast. It was difficult to know just how she was taking this little homily, but at least she was not reacting violently. Hilda thanked her stars that Winifred had always been a placid girl. Some daughters would have answered back, or burst into tears, or flounced from the room, thought Hilda with relief.

'And you think Leslie will lose interest in me too?' queried the girl quietly.

'That's up to you,' responded Hilda. 'You certainly shouldn't encourage him. You don't want to find yourself married to a Howard, I hope.'

'Why not?' asked Winnie, setting the jug carefully on a shelf. Her back was towards her mother, so that Hilda could not see her face, but her voice was as calm as ever.

'Why not?' echoed Hilda, now too confidently embarked upon her mission. 'Because your father and I have hopes of something better for you than becoming a baker's wife when you decide to get married. We've always done our very best to introduce you to nice families. You can look higher than the Howards for a husband. Surely you can see that?'

The girl wheeled round and the determined look upon her face shook her mother into silence.

'There's one thing I can see,' said Winnie levelly, 'and that is that I've got a snob for a mother.' And before Hilda could get her breath back, Winnie walked, head-high and unhurried, from the room.

It was not only Hilda who had been perturbed by the fast-growing attachment between Leslie and Winnie. Bertie too had watched the pair with misgivings quite as strong, but of quite a different nature. His affection for the Howard boys was unchanged by the years. He was now approaching twenty-one, a thoughtful, intelligent young man, but still harbouring traces of that hero-worship he had felt as a child for the two boys who were his seniors. Jim at twenty-four, and Leslie at twenty-two, seemed to be grown men, and Leslie certainly was experienced in the ways of women. Bertie, of shyer disposition, felt that he knew too little of the world to question the Howards' actions. Nevertheless, his deep affection for Winnie put him on his guard, and he observed her growing awareness of Leslie's charms with uneasiness.

If Jim had been Winnie's choice, Bertie would have been delighted. Bertie and Jim had much in common, both being peace-loving young men, thoroughly engrossed in their jobs and enjoying the pleasant social life of Caxley in their spare time. There was a steadiness about Jim which Leslie lacked. He might be incapable of sweeping a girl off her feet, but he would make a thoroughly reliable husband. Bertie, inexperienced as he was, could not fail to see that Leslie might prove far too volatile for such a lasting institution as marriage.

But this was not the only thing which worried Bertie. He knew, only too well, that there was a streak of cruelty in Leslie. There had been birds' nesting expeditions, when they were boys, when Jim and Bertie had seen Leslie throw a young bird wantonly over a hedge. Bertie had once come upon Leslie in the baker's yard chastizing their old spaniel with unnecessary severity because it had chased a cat. Both Bertie and Jim had made their disgust plain on these occasions, but Leslie appeared unrepentant. Bertie himself remembered many a twisted arm and painful kick delivered by Leslie, for no apparent reason but self-indulgence. As he grew older, and enjoyed his successes with the girls, the same callousness showed in his attitude to those of whom he had tired. He showed not a quiver of compunction. For Leslie, when the affair was done, it was finished completely, and he passed to his next willing victim without one glance behind. It was small wonder that Bertie trembled for Winnie, so young and so vulnerable. Should he say anything to her, he wondered? Or would it simply add fuel to the fire?

He salved his conscience with the thought that almost always the pair were in company with other young people. Besides, Winnie was a sensible girl and had known Leslie and his ways long enough to realize that his affection would certainly not last long. He decided that it would be prudent to keep silence.

Other matters engaged Bertie's attention at this time, distracting him from the affairs of his sister. Kathy Howard, now nineteen and working in the family business, had long been taken for granted by Bertie as an occasional tennis partner or a useful team member when they played 'Clumps' at parties. But during the summer of 1913 Bertie began to find her presence curiously and delightfully disturbing. She was as vividly beautiful as her mother had been at the same age, and attracted as much attention from the boys. Her hair was a dusky cloud, her eyes large and luminous. She could dance all night without flagging, and had a gay recklessness which, until now, Bertie had dismissed as 'showing off'. When young Mary North, aged eight, had dared her to jump from their garden bridge fully clothed into the Cax, Kathy had done so immediately, and been reproved by Bertie. When the attic curtains blew out from the windows, high above the market square, and became caught in the guttering, it was Kathy who stood on the window-sill to release them before the three boys had pounded up the stairs after her. And it was Bertie again who remonstrated with her.

But these things had happened a year or two earlier, before Bertie's feelings had suffered a change. The very thought now of the risks that Kathy ran made Bertie tremble with apprehension. She was becoming incredibly precious to him, he realized with surprise. Meanwhile, oblivious of his feelings, Kathy continued her carelessly happy way, as dazzling as a butterfly, flitting from one pleasure to the next, with no thought of settling down. And Bertie was content to watch her with increasing delight, and to accustom himself to these new tremors which her presence excited.

He had another cause for concern. He strongly suspected that things were not well with the family finances and only wished he could ask his father openly about the situation. Somehow, it was not easy to speak to him. Bertie awaited an opportunity, half-hoping, half-fearing that his father would broach the subject, but time passed and nothing was said. It did not escape Bertie's notice, however, that his father was more preoccupied than usual, and that some of the stock was not being replaced when it was sold. He had a pretty shrewd idea that Tenby's had hit his father's trade more seriously than he would admit.

Nevertheless, the staff still numbered six, presumably were being paid, and were content with their lot. Bob, who had been at North's since leaving school, was now head assistant and Bender left more and more responsibility to him. He had grown into a harassed vague individual with a walrus moustache. His steel-rimmed spectacles screened myopic brown eyes which peered dazedly at the world about him. Despite his unprepossessing appearance the customers liked him and the staff treated him with deference. Unmarried, he lived with his old mother and seemed to have no particular vices, unless whist at the working men's club, and occasional bets on a horse, could be counted against him. Poor, plain Miss Taggerty, who was in charge of the kitchen ware at North's, openly adored him, fluttering her meagre sandy eyelashes, and displaying her distressingly protruding teeth and pink gums, in vast smiles which Bob appeared not to see. Only the very lowliest member of North's staff, young Tim, aged thirteen, sniggered at Miss Taggerty's fruitless endeavours and was soundly cuffed by the other assistants when so discovered. To them, disrespect towards Bob was tantamount to disrespect to Bender and the family. If Bob seemed satisfied with conditions in the business, Bertie told himself, why should he perturb himself unduly?

Summer slid into autumn, and the picnics and river parties gave way to concerts and dances as the days drew in. It was in October that the Caxley Orchestra gave its grandest concert each year, and in 1913 Winnie North appeared for the first time among the violinists.

Her family turned up in full force to do her honour. They sat in the front row of the balcony at the Corn Exchange.

'In case Mary wants to go out during the performance – you know what she is,' said her mother.

Mary, dressed in white silk with a wide sash of red satin, was beside herself with excitement. This was better than going to bed! Her eyes sparkled as she gazed about the crowded hall. Hilda, matronly in black velvet, did her best to quell her youngest's volatile spirits. Bender, at the end of the row, smiled indulgently upon his handsome family and their friends.

For the Howard family had been invited to join the party, and although Sep and Edna had excused themselves, and their youngest was in bed with the mumps, yet Leslie and Kathy were present and were to take Winnie and Bertie to their home for supper after the show.

As the performance went on the air grew warmer and more soporific in the balcony. Bertie found his attention wandering as the orchestra ploughed its way valiantly through Mozart's 'Eine Kleine Nachtmusik'. Along the row he could see Kathy's bronze leather shoe, wagging in time with the music, beneath the hem of her yellow skirt. Below the balcony, ranged neatly in rows each side of the wide gangway he could see the heads of almost two hundred worthy Caxley folk.

There was the mayor's bald pate, shining and pink, gleaming in the front row. Beside him were the glossy black locks, suspiciously lacking any silvery flecks or light and shade, of his sixty-year-old wife. Near him Bertie could see the bent figure of old Sir James Diller from Beech Green, his ear trumpet well in evidence and his shaking head cocked to hear every indistinct sound. Immediately behind him sat his manservant, ready to aid his ageing master if need be. In the same row were the manservant's sister and her husband, the local butcher, there to hear their two sons performing, one as a flautist and the other as a violinist.

Bertie's eyes wandered farther afield. There was the postmaster, whose son had just lost a leg as the result of a train accident. There was the cobbler who drank, the schoolmistress who sang like an angel and the elderly curate of St Peter's who was father-confessor to half the parish. There was Mrs Gadd, the watchmaker's wife, who was aunt to Bob at the shop, and refused to have anything to do with him, for reasons unknown, and always demanded to be served by Bender himself. There was her cousin, known to young Caxleyites as 'old Scabby' because of his unfortunate complexion, and the chastiser of Bertie, aged six, when he had trespassed into the old man's garden in search of a lost ball. And beyond him was Louisa Howard, aunt to Kathy, and a thorn in the side of the Howard family because of her rebellious ways. Her flaming red hair and flaming red nose matched the flaming temper which scorched all with whom she came in contact.

'A vixen,' Bender called her, 'and a vicious vixen at that. If she'd been a boy she'd have been packed off to sea.'

Bertie's eyes strayed back to the platform. Husbands, wives, sons, and daughters, nieces and nephews scraped and blew, banged and squealed to the pride of their relatives in the audience. Bertie watched his sister's smooth fair head bent above her violin. Her pretty plump arm sawed energetically up and down as she concentrated on the music propped up before her.

How closely they were all tied, thought Bertie! Not only by the bonds of kinship which enlaced most of those in the Corn Exchange, but also by the bonds of shared experience. They not only knew each other, their faults and their foibles, they shared the town of Caxley. They knew the most sheltered spot to stand in the market square when the easterly wind blew sharp and keen across the cobbles. They knew where the biggest puddles had to be dodged on dark nights, and where the jasmine smelt sweetest on a summer evening. They knew where the trout rose in the Cax, where a nightingale could be heard and where lovers could wander undisturbed. They knew who sold the freshest meat, and who the stalest. They knew who made the stoutest boots, the smartest frocks and the best pork pies. In short, they were as closely knit as a family, and as lucky as villagers in a village, in that Caxley was small enough, and leisurely enough too, for them to appreciate each other and the little town which was home to them all.

Nodding gently, in the pleasant stuffiness of the balcony, Bertie gazed through half-closed eyes at his fellow-citizens and found them good.

Some chaps, mused Bertie to himself, would be itching to get away from all this at my age, but Caxley suits me!

He caught sight of Kathy's tapping toe again and sat up straight.

Yes, Caxley would certainly suit him, he decided, as 'Eine Kleine Nachtmusik' crashed triumphantly to a close, and he joined enthusiastically in Caxley's generous, and wholly biased, applause.

8. A Trip to Beech Green

WINNIE was flushed with excitement after the performance. Bertie had never seen her looking so pretty, nor had Leslie, it was plain.

They sat at the Howards' supper table and Bertie, hungry after three hours of Caxley music, looked with pleasure at the magnificent pork pie which stood before Sep at one end of the table, and the huge bowl of salad before Edna at the other. One of Sep's superb bread rolls, with a carefully plaited top, lay on each side plate, and Bertie broke his in two, savouring its delicious scent.

'Let us call a blessing on the food,' intoned Sep sonorously, and Bertie hastily put his erring hands in his lap and bent his shamed head. It was bad enough to look greedy. It looked even worse to appear irreverent. Cursing his luck, Bertie could only hope that the whole table had not seen his actions. But, catching the eye of Winnie across the table, he soon saw that one member of the family would tell the tale against him later on.

'Lord bless this food to our use and us to Thy service,' droned Sep, his thin hands pressed together and eyes tightly shut.

'Amen,' murmured the rest of them, and there was an uncomfortable silence, broken at last by Sep himself who picked up a large knife and fork flanking the pie and began to cut the golden crust, with almost as much reverence as his saying of grace.

Bertie, anxious to reinstate himself, passed the butter dish to Edna and complimented her on the superb vase of late roses which were the centrepiece of the table.

'Your ma gave them to me,' replied Edna. Bertie fell silent and studied the tablecloth.

It was a white damask one similar to those used in the North household, but much greyer, and badly ironed. Bertie could not imagine his mother allowing such a cloth on their own table, and certainly not such thick white plates, chipped here and there, and covered with minute cracks across the glaze where they had been left too long to heat in the oven. His knife blade wobbled on its handle, and the tines of his fork were so worn that it was difficult to spear the slippery pieces of tomato on his plate. He wondered why Sep and Edna endured such shabby adjuncts to their superb food, and also, as a rich crumb of pastry fell into his lap, why they did not think to provide table napkins. But it was positively churlish, he told himself, to think in this way at his host's table, and he set himself out to draw Edna into conversation about young Robert's mumps. He felt Kathy's eyes upon him across the table, and hoped she did not think too badly of his early gaffe.

'It's a funny thing,' Edna began energetically, 'but one side of his neck don't hardly notice, but the other's up like a football. Of course he can't swallow a thing, and his poor head's that hot you could poach an egg on it!'

Once launched, Edna sailed along readily enough, and Bertie allowed his mind to wander.

Only Winnie seemed to sparkle and Leslie too was at his gayest. Their end of the table, where Sep presided, seemed considerably livelier than Edna's where Bertie was doing his best to woo the subject from infectious diseases, but with small success. Edna had no small talk, and, as Dan Crockford had found years before, very little of interest in her beautiful head. But she liked to chatter, and the subject of mumps had led, naturally enough, to measles, whooping cough, diphtheria and other children's ailments which had caused Edna dramatic alarm over the years.

'And that young Dr Martin, who's gone over to Fairacre now – and a good thing too if you ask me – he came and had a look at our Leslie. And I said to him: "He's got yellow jaundice, doctor," and do you know what he said?'

Bertie murmured politely.

'He simply said: "And how do you know?" With that poor little ha'porth as yellow as a guinea! It didn't need much to tell a mother what was wrong with him, but doctors don't give no one any credit for having a bit of sense. Though I must say, speaking fair, he give Leslie some very strong medicine, which did him a world of good.'

She gazed down the table at her second-born, and sighed happily.

'Make a lovely couple, don't they?' she said artlessly, and Bertie felt his heart sink. Was it really becoming so obvious to everyone? Could it be that a marriage would be arranged between the two? Bertie felt cold at the thought, and even Kathy's smiles and cheerful conversation after supper could not quite dispel the chill at his heart.

They made their farewells soon after eleven and emerged into the quiet market square. The stars shone brightly from a clear sky above the tumbled Caxley roofs. In the yard of the public house a horse snorted, as it awaited its master. A few late home-goers straggled past Queen Victoria's upright figure, and somewhere, in the distance, a cat yowled in a dark alley.

Leslie had accompanied them down the stairs and opened the door at the side of the shop for them.

'Goodnight, Leslie, and thank you again,' said Bertie. But Leslie was not listening. Bertie saw that his hand held Winnie's tightly, and that the two were exchanging a look of complete love and understanding.

The Norths crossed the square, turned to wave to Leslie silhouetted against the light from his open door, and entered their own home.

Bertie made his way to bed that night with much food for thought.

It was soon after this that Bertie acquired his first motor-car, and it did much to distract the young man from his cares. It was a small two-seater, an A.C. Sociable, by name, and had been owned by young Tenby, the son of the flourishing ironmonger in Caxley High Street, since 1909 when it was in its first glory. Young Tenby, now married, with one son and another expected, had bought a larger car. It was the envy of all Caxley, a glossy new Lanchester, and Bertie was able to buy the old one at a very favourable price. One of his first trips was to Beech Green to take his mother to visit Ethel, now happily married to Jesse Miller, and also awaiting the birth of her second child.

Hilda, her hat tied on with a becoming grey motoring veil, sat very upright beside Bertie trying to hide her apprehension. But once the terrors of Caxley High Street were past, and they entered the leafy lane which climbed from the Cax valley to the downs beyond, her fears were calmed, and she looked about her at the glowing autumn trees with excited pleasure. Speech was well-nigh impossible because of noise and dust, but once they had drawn up, with a flourish, outside the farmhouse door, she complimented Bertie on his driving.

'Thank you, mamma,' said Bertie, secretly amused, 'but it's what I've been doing ever since I left school you know. I'm glad you weren't too frightened.'

While the two sisters exchanged news, Jesse Miller took Bertie round the farm. Harvest was over early that year and the stubble in Hundred Acre Field glittered like a golden sea. The two men crunched their way across it, Bertie envying his uncle's leather leggings which protected his legs from the sharp straw which pricked unmercifully through his own socks. He was glad when they approached the hedge of a cottage garden and Jesse paused to speak to the family who were working there. He bent down and removed some of the cruellest of the tormentors from the tops of his boots and his socks, and caught a glimpse through the bare hedge of a pretty girl, with her father, and a tall young man with red hair.

'Our thatcher,' said Jesse Miller, as they resumed their tour of the farm. 'Francis Clare. Just had to let him know the barn roof needs patching after last week-end's gale.'

'And the girl?'

'Dolly, his daughter. And the copper-nob's her young man, Arnold Fletcher. Getting married next year, I hear. Time you thought of it yourself, Bertie.'

'I'll remember,' promised Bertie.

The air was pure and refreshing, up here on the downs, and scented with the sweet-sad smells of autumn, the damp earth underfoot, and the dying bracken growing in the rustling hedge. Bertie paused to look about him in this lovely open place. In the Cax valley such exhilaration rarely seized him. There was something strong and uplifting in the great sweep of hills with the moving clouds gliding across their tops. He would like to live here, savouring their tranquillity, one day. Perhaps with Kathy for company, he wondered? The thought was as heady as the winds about him.

They returned to the farmhouse for a gigantic tea. A bowlful of freshly boiled brown eggs, set in the centre of the table, was only a prelude to the ham sandwiches, hot buttered scones, home made plum jam, Victoria sponge, Dundee cake, custard tartlets, and half a dozen dishes of assorted small cakes.

Ethel pressed her sister and nephew to eat heartily as they had such a long cold drive before them, and Hilda returned the compliment by persuading Ethel to eat equally well as she was 'feeding two'. Between them they managed to dispatch quite half the food arrayed on the table before setting off for home behind the hissing acetylene lamps.

Half-way between Beech Green and Caxley, a fine hare leapt from a high bank and zig-zagged along the road in front of the car, bewildered by the lights. Bertie slowed down and it stopped. He moved gently forward again and the hare continued its erratic and terrified course. At length, Hilda could bear it no longer, and motioned Bertie to stop completely, which he did in a convenient farm gateway.

The hare made off across the fields. It was very quiet with the engine at rest, and Hilda gave a little sigh.

'Bertie,' she began, 'we don't often get a little time on our own, and before we get home I want your advice.'

'My advice?' queried Bertie, genuinely startled. 'It's usually the other way round, mamma.'

'I'm worried about so many things, Bertie, and I can't discuss them all with your father. Winnie and Leslie Howard is one worry, and there's another.'

She stopped, and her voice had a little tremor which did not escape Bertie.

'There's not much one can do about Winnie,' said he gently. 'She's got plenty of sense, and father will surely have a word with Leslie if he's worried.'

'I doubt it,' responded Hilda, with a flash of spirit. 'He's got worries of his own, I suspect, which are more serious than he'll admit to me.'

She turned to him suddenly.

'Bertie, do try and talk to him. You're a man now, and can help. Something's going very wrong with the business, and he won't discuss it with me. But he's getting so unusually tight with money these days, and only this morning he said he didn't think we'd have the staff Christmas party.'

'No party?' echoed Bertie. Things must be serious indeed if this annual jollity, which Bender so much enjoyed, were to be cancelled.

'And there's a lot of other things. This car, for instance. He's really cross that you've bought it, and says we can't afford it.'

'But it's my own money,' protested Bertie, with justifiable heat. 'I saved every penny of it! Father knows that! And in any case, it's a dashed sight cheaper to run this little A.C. than to keep our horses in fodder and the trap in repair. Really, it's a bit thick!'

'Forget what I said,' said Hilda hastily, patting her son's hand. 'It's simply that he's terribly worried, and if you can help him, Bertie, he'll be so grateful, and so will I.'

'I'll do what I can, mamma,' replied Bertie, a trifle huffily, starting up the car again.

He drove home, fuming secretly at his father's criticism. Can't afford it indeed! Anyone would think he'd badgered the old man into parting with his money! For two pins he'd have it out with him the minute he got home!

But the words were never said. For when he and his mother entered the drawing-room above the shop, they found Bender white-faced, his sparse hair on end, and papers and account books in confusion on the desk and floor.

'Bender,' cried Hilda, hurrying towards him, 'what on earth has happened?'

'Plenty!' replied Bender grimly. 'Bob's gone off with the cash box, and I've sent the police after him!'

9. *Thoughts in the Snow*

THE news of Bob's disappearance swept through Caxley with the speed and commotion of a forest fire.

'I've never liked the look of that fellow,' wheezed fat Mrs Petty, wise after the event. 'Had a look in his eye like this 'ere cod. Proper slimy customer, I always thought.'

The square buzzed with the gossip on that market day. Both stallholders and customers knew Bob and Bender well. It seemed a shameful thing for a man to serve his master so shabbily, wagged some of the tongues.

'We ain't heard Bob's side yet,' replied the more cautious. 'Catch the fellow first, I says. Maybe 'e never took it after all. Who's to say?'

As soon as Sep Howard heard of the affair he went across the square to see Bender. He did not relish the encounter. Bender hurt could be Bender at his most truculent, as Sep well knew, and the age-long tremors still shook the little man as he entered the ironmonger's shop.

Bender was rummaging in one of the many small drawers ranged on the wall behind the counter.

'Can you spare a minute?' asked Sep.

Bender led the way, without a word, into the shop parlour behind the shop, where private transactions were carried out. He motioned Sep to a high office stool and sat himself heavily on another.

'S'pose you've heard?' grunted Bender. 'Fine old how-d'you-do, ain't it?'

'I'm sorry,' said Sep. 'Was much taken?'

'The week's takings.'

Sep drew in his breath with a hiss. He knew what it was to face such disasters in business.

'Any chance of getting it back?'

'I doubt it, Sep, I doubt it.' Bender passed a gigantic hand over his face and head, as though to wipe away the cares that clung to him. 'There's no doubt about one thing though. The blighter's been helping himself off and on for two or three months now, and I hadn't twigged. Been too careless by half, Sep. Left too much to him, you see.'

He pushed a ledger across to him.

'See that eight? That was a three. See that nine? That was a nought. Oh, he's been having a high old time among the books just lately!'

'But what's behind it? He got a decent wage, lived pretty small, never seemed to flash the money about.'

'Betting,' said Bender briefly. 'Always liked a bob on a horse, and now it's turned into a sovereign. I've been round to see his old ma, and it all came out. I feel sorry for the poor old girl, I must say. Come to that, I feel pretty sorry for myself, Sep.'

This seemed Sep's chance to speak up, and he took it.

'If I can help, I hope you'll let me. I don't forget all you did for me, you know. You gave me a hand when I needed it most and I'd like to have the chance to help, if there's any mortal way of doing it.'

Bender's great face flushed red. There was no doubt that he was touched by the offer. He cleared his throat huskily before answering.

'Good of you, Sep. I appreciate it very much, and you'd be the first I'd turn to, if it came to it. But I ain't pushed for a pound yet, and I reckon North's will make it, Bob or no Bob.'

There was a heartiness about this reply which did not ring quite true to Sep. Bender was making light of a situation which was far more serious than he would admit. But Sep could do no more in the circumstances.

'Well, I'll be over the way if you want me any time,

Bender. You know that. I hope it'll all get cleared up satisfactorily.'

He made his way from the shop feeling very worried. But in the midst of his doubts and fears, he took comfort from the words still ringing in his ears.

'You'd be the first I'd turn to, if it came to it!'

He never thought to hear Bender North utter those words to him.

A week passed, and still the villain was at large. The police had found that he was seen on the London-bound train on the evening of his disappearance. Two Caxley ladies, returning from a day's shopping in town, also remembered seeing him at Paddington station. Beyond that, there was nothing. Somewhere, Bob was lying very quietly indeed, waiting for the hue and cry to die down, it seemed.

It was almost November and a bitingly cold east wind bedevilled the town, raising tempers as well as dust. Doors banged, windows rattled, and fires smoked indoors. Outdoors it was even worse. The wind whipped off hats, stung cheeks, inflamed eyes, and screamed through the awnings of the market stalls. Dust eddied in miniature whirlwinds, raising paper, leaves, and straw, and depositing them where they were least wanted. Coughs and colds, sore throats and chapped lips plagued the populace, and it was generally agreed that it would be 'a darned good thing when the wind changed'.

Unscathed by the hostile world about them, Leslie and Winnie continued to rejoice in each other's company. Bertie had dutifully spoken to his sister, saying that their mother was worried, and that he too hoped that she was not serious about Leslie. Winnie had answered briefly. They had known the Howards all their lives. She knew what she was doing. She also knew that her mother was worried, and they had spoken about it before Bertie was approached. Bertie, having fired his warning shot, retreated in some disarray before Winnie's level defence.

Sep had suddenly realized what was afoot and secretly approved of their union. What could be more fitting than a wedding between the two families? It would be a happy bond between Bender and himself. He recalled Bender's comforting words. Sep's heart warmed to the young people. His Leslie was a fine boy and it was time he settled down. Winnie would make a good wife. As far as Sep could see the outlook was rosy. He liked the idea of the young couple finding happiness together. He liked too the idea of becoming closer to Bender. He said as much to Edna, and was disconcerted by her reply.

'You don't think *he'll* like it, do you? Nor our Hilda! She's got her eye on the gentry for her Winnie! Nothing less than a belted earl for Hilda's daughter!'

'What's wrong with Leslie? Fine upstanding youngster with a share in the business – you don't tell me that the Norths will disapprove?'

'That I do!' responded Edna flatly. 'Say what you like, Sep, the Norths have always looked down on us, and they won't let their Winnie marry Leslie without a fight.'

'You're fancying things!' muttered Sep, turning away. There was too much truth in Edna's sallies to please him, but he refused to be daunted.

'Let the young 'uns find their own way,' he pronounced at last, and hurried into the bakery before he heard any more unwelcome home truths.

There was plenty of work to distract Sep's attention from his son's affairs of the heart during the next few weeks, for Christmas was approaching, and there were scores of Christmas cakes to be made and iced.

Although Sep now employed several more workers, he still did as much himself in the bakery. The fragrance of the rich mixture, the mingled aroma of spices, candied fruits, and brown sugar, cheered Sep afresh every year. It was his own personal offering to the spirit of Christmas, and he enjoyed the festive bustle in the warmly scented bakery. It was like a sheltered haven from the bleak winds in the market square beyond the doors.

The cold spell was lasting longer than expected, and the weather-wise old folk prophesied a white Christmas in Caxley. Sure enough, in the week before Christmas, a light fall whitened the ground and powdered the rosy-tiled roofs of the town, and the lowering grey skies told of more to follow.

On Sunday afternoon, Bender set off for Beech Green with two large saw blades for Jesse Miller.

'He won't get much done in the fields,' commented Bender wrapping the blades briskly in brown paper. 'The ground's like iron. He'll be glad to set the men to sawing firewood tomorrow, and I promised him these as soon as they came.'

'Give them all my love,' said Hilda. 'I won't come with you with the weather like this. And wrap up warmly, do, my dear. Put your muffler on, and your thick gloves.'

'Never fear,' answered Bender robustly. 'I've known the downs long enough to know how to dress for them. I'll be back before dark.'

The horse trotted briskly through the town. There were very few people about and Bender was glad to be on his own, in the clean fresh air. Now he could turn over his thoughts, undisturbed by family interruptions or customers' problems. He always felt at his best driving behind a good horse. He liked the rhythm of its flying feet, the gay rattle of the bowling wheels, and the clink and squeak of the well-polished harness.

The pace slackened as Bill, the horse, approached Beech Green. The long pull up the downs was taken gently and steadily. The reins lay loosely across the glossy back, and

Bender reviewed his situation as they jogged along together through the grey and white countryside.

Things were serious, that was plain. Bob had been picked up by the London police ten days earlier, and now awaited his trial at the next Assizes. He had been in possession of fourteen shillings and ninepence at the time of his arrest, and could not – or would not – give any idea of where the rest of the money had gone. Clearly, nothing would be restored to his employer.

What would he do, Bender asked himself? He could get a further loan from the bank, but would it be of any use? Had the time come to take a partner who would be willing to put money into the firm? Bender disliked the idea. He could approach both Sep Howard and Jesse Miller who had offered help, but he hated the thought of letting Sep Howard see his straits, and he doubted whether Jesse Miller could afford to give him the sum needed to give the business a fresh start. Jesse was in partnership with his brother Harry at the farm, and times were hard for them both at the moment.

The other course was a much more drastic one. Tenby's had approached him with a tentative offer. If he ever decided to part with the business would he give them first offer? He would of course be offered a post with the firm who would be glad of his experience. They were thinking of housing their agricultural machinery department on separate premises. North's, in the market square, handy for all the farmers in the district, would suit them perfectly. They asked Bender to bear it in mind. Bender had thought of little else for two days, but had said nothing to Hilda. He knew well enough that she would be all in favour of the action, and he wanted to be sure that it was right before making any final decisions. Hilda, for years now, had been pressing Bender to move from the shop to one of the new houses on the hill at the south side of the town.

'It's so much healthier for the children,' asserted Hilda.

'You know how chesty Mary is – she takes after you, you know – and it's so damp right by the river here.'

'She looks all right to me,' Bender said.

'Besides,' continued his wife, changing her tactics, 'everyone's moving away from the businesses – the Loaders, the Ashtons, the Percys –'

'The Howards aren't,' pointed out Bender. Hilda tossed her head impatiently.

'Don't be awkward, Bender! Who cares what the Howards do anyway? It would be far better for Bertie and Winnie, and Mary too, later on, to have a place they can ask their friends to without feeling ashamed.'

'Ashamed?' echoed Bender thunderously. 'What's wrong with this place?'

'We could have a tennis court if we had a bigger garden,' said Hilda. Her blue eyes held that far-away look which Bender had come to realize was the prelude to some expense or another. 'The children could invite all sorts of nice people to tennis parties.'

'They're free to invite them here to parties – boating and otherwise – as far as I'm concerned,' said Bender. 'Don't tell me that it's the children who want to move. It's entirely your notion, my dear, and a mighty expensive one too.'

Hilda had fallen silent after that, but returned to the attack many times until Bender had begun to wonder if there was something in the idea after all. It was not social progress, though, that caused Bender to give the matter his attention, but the financial possibilities of the move.

If Tenby's made him the substantial offer he expected, he could well afford to buy Hilda the house of her dreams. There was no doubt about it that the market place living quarters were rambling and far too large for their needs. Bertie and Winnie, it was reasonable to suppose, would be married and away before long. It would be more economical, in every way, for those who were left, to live in a smaller and more up-to-date house where repairs and upkeep would probably be less than half the present sum. Also, Hilda was right in saying that they would find it healthier. Not only would they be on higher ground; it would be a good thing to leave the business behind at night and get right away from its responsibilities.

He presumed that he would be offered the managership. In that case there would be a steady income, with no worries attached. Bender, gazing unseeingly across the snowy fields, lulled almost into slumber by the rhythmic swaying of the trap, began to feel that selling North's might be the best way out of his many difficulties. But not yet, he told himself. He would hang on as long as he could, and who knows? Something might turn up. He'd been lucky often enough before. There was still hope! Bender North was always an optimist.

He put Billy into the shelter of a stable and tramped across the snowy yard to the Millers' back door.

He was greeted warmly by the family, and he was put by the fire to thaw out. The usual vast tea was offered him, but Bender ate sparingly, with one eye cocked on the grey threatening sky outside.

'I mustn't be too long,' said Bender, his mouth full of buttered toast. 'There's more snow to come before morning, or I'll eat my boots.'

They exchanged family news. Ethel's youngest was running a temperature, and was upstairs in bed, 'very fretful and scratchity', as his mother said. Jesse's pigs were not doing as well as he had hoped, and he had an idea that one of his men was taking eggs. 'Times were bad enough for farmers,' said Jesse, 'without such set-backs.'

He accompanied Bender to the stable when he set off.

'And how are your affairs?' he asked when they were out of earshot of the house. Bender gave a reassuring laugh, and clapped the other man's shoulders.

'Better than they have been, Jesse, I'm glad to say. I hope I shan't have to worry you at all.'

The look of relief that flooded Jesse's face did not escape Bender. It certainly looked as though Tenby's would be the only possible avenue of escape if the business grew worse.

Ah well, thought Bender, clattering across the cobbled yard, we must just live in hope of something turning up! He waved to Jesse and set off at a spanking pace on the downhill drive home.

The snow began to fall as Bender turned out of Jesse's gate. It came down thickly and softly, large flakes flurrying across mile upon mile of open downland, like an undulating lacy curtain. It settled rapidly upon the iron-hard ground, already sheeted in the earlier fall, and by the time Billy had covered half a mile the sound of his trotting hoofs was muffled. He snorted fiercely at the onslaught of this strange element, his breath bursting from his flaring nostrils in clouds of vapour. His dark mane was starred with snow flakes, and as he tossed his head Bender caught a glimpse of his shining eyes grotesquely ringed with glistening snow caught in his eyelashes.

His own face was equally assaulted. The snow flakes fluttered against his lips and eyes like icy moths. It was difficult to breathe. He pulled down the brim of his hard hat, and hoisted up the muffler that Hilda had insisted on his wearing, so that he could breathe in the stuffy pocket of air made by his own warmth. Already the front of his coat was plastered, and he looked like a snowman.

A flock of sheep, in a field, huddled together looking like one vast fleece ribbed with snow. The bare hedges were fast becoming blanketed, and the banks undulated past the bowling trap smoothly white, but for the occasional pock-mark of a bird's claws. The tall dry grasses bore strange exotic white flowers in their dead heads, and the branches of trees collected snowy burdens in their arms.

And all the time there was a rustling and whispering, a sibilance of snow. The air was alive with movement, the dancing and whirling of a thousand thousand individual flakes with a life as brief as the distance from leaden sky to frozen earth. At the end of their tempestuous short existence they lay together, dead and indivisible, forming a common shroud.

There was a grandeur and beauty about this snowy countryside which affected Bender deeply. Barns and houses, woods and fields were now only massive white shapes, their angles smoothed into gentle curves. He passed a cow-man returning from milking, his head and shoulders shrouded in a sack, shaped like a monk's cowl. He was white from head to foot, only his dark eyes, glancing momentarily at the passing horse, and his plodding gait distinguished him from the white shapes about him.

Bender turned to watch him vanishing into the veil of swirling flakes. Behind him, the wheels were spinning out two grey ribbons, along the snowy road. He doubted whether they would still be visible to the fellow traveller, so fast were they being covered from above.

He turned back and flicked the reins on Billy's snow-spattered satin back.

'Gee up, boy!' roared Bender cheerfully. 'We both want to get home!'

Sep Howard watched the snow falling from his bedroom window. His hair was rumpled from a rare afternoon nap on the bed, and he had awakened to find the window darkened with flying flakes.

He judged that it was two or three inches deep already. The steps of St Peter's and the Town Hall were heavily carpeted. The snow had blown into the cracks and jambs of doors and windows, leaving long white sticks like newly-spilt milk. A mantle of snow draped Queen Victoria's shoulders and her bronze crown supported a little white cushion which looked like ermine. Snow lay along her sceptre and in the folds of her robes. The iron cups, in the fountain at her feet, were filled to the brim with snow flakes, and the embossed lions near by peered from snow-encrusted manes.

There were very few people about for a Sunday afternoon. An old tramp, carrying his belongings in a red-spotted bundle on a stick, shuffled disconsolately past St Peter's, head bent, rheumy eyes fixed upon the snow at his feet. Two ragged urchins, no doubt from the marsh, giggled and barged each other behind him, scraping up the snow in red, wet hands to make snowballs.

Sep watched them heave them at the back of the unsuspecting old man. At the moment of impact he swung round sharply, and raised his bundle threateningly. Sep could see his red, wet, toothless mouth protesting, but could hear no word through the tightly-shut bedroom window. One boy put his thumb to his nose impudently: the other put out his tongue. But they let the old man shuffle round the corner unmolested before throwing their arms round each other's skinny shoulders and running jubilantly down an alley-way.

Momentarily the market square was empty. Not even a pigeon pattered across the snow. Only footprints of various sizes, and the yellow stain made by a horse's urine, gave any sign of life in that white world. Snow clothed the rosy bricks and sloping roofs of Caxley. It covered the hanging signs and the painted nameboards above the shops, dousing the bright colours as a candle snuffer douses a light.

What a grey and white world, thought Sep! As grey and white as an old gander, as grey and white as the swans and cygnets floating together on the Cax! The railings outside the bank stood starkly etched against the white background, each spear-top tipped with snow. There was something very soothing in this negation of colour and movement. It reminded Sep of creeping beneath the bedclothes as a child, and crouching there, in a soft, white haven, unseeing and unseen, all sounds muffled, as he relished the secrecy and security of it all.

There was a movement in St Peter's porch and a dozen or so choirboys came tumbling out into the snowy world, released from carol practice. The sight brought Sep, sighing, back into the world of Sunday afternoon.

He picked up a hair-brush and began to attack his tousled locks.

'Looks as though the weather prophets are right,' said Sep to his reflection. 'Caxley's in for a white Christmas this year.'

10. *Trouble at North's*

THE weather prophets were right. Caxley had a white Christmas and the good people of the town walked to church and chapel through a sugar-icing world sparkling in bright sunshine.

Edna, wrapped warmly in a new black coat trimmed with fur at the neck and hem – Sep's Christmas present to her – felt snug and happy, as she composed herself to day-dreaming whilst the minister delivered his half-hour's exhortation. Even his stern countenance was a little softened by the joyous festival, she noticed.

'New hope, a new life, a New Year,' declaimed the minister, and Edna thought how queer it would be to write 1914 so soon. It would be a relief too, in a way. She had felt a little uneasy throughout 1913. It was an unlucky number. Gipsy superstitions played a larger part in Edna's life than ever her husband suspected.

Yes, there was something reassuring about the sound of 1914. She was going to enjoy this beautiful Christmas and her beautiful new coat, and look forward to an even more prosperous New Year than ever before!

'Peace on earth, goodwill toward men,' the minister was saying, one finger upraised for attention.

Edna stroked her new fur trimming and sighed contentedly.

Hilda North also welcomed the New Year. In its early months Bender, with his mind now clear, told her of Tenby's offer and the possibility of buying the house of her dreams on Caxley's southern slopes.

Hilda was joyful and triumphant.

'Have you told Bertie?' was her first question. 'He ought to know. After all, this would have been his one day.'

Bender promised to speak to his son that evening. It was a mild spring day with soft rain falling, straight and steady over Caxley and the countryside. In his waterside garden, Bender watched the rain collecting in the cups of his fine red tulips, and dripping, drop by drop, from leaf to leaf, down the japonica bush against the workshop wall. The Cax was dimpled with rain, the rustic bridge glistened. There was a soft freshness in the whispering air that soothed, and yet saddened, the watching man. He was going to miss all this, after so many years. Would Bertie miss it too?

Bertie, at that moment, was also watching the rain. He was at Fairacre where he had been summoned by old Mr Parr whose automobile refused to start. Bertie had spent the morning repairing it, and now sat in the thatched barn which housed the car, munching a sausage roll which was his lunch. A robin splashed in a puddle near by, flirting wings and tail, bobbing its thumb-sized head, as it gloried in its bath.

A veil of drops fell steadily from the thatched roof, splashing on to the washed gravel surrounding the building. In the field next door Bertie could see sheep moving slowly and unconcernedly, their wool soaked with rain. Steam gently rose from their backs as they cropped. An old cart-horse, streaked with the wet, nodded under a horse chestnut tree, its back as shiny as the sticky buds bursting from the branches above it.

It was a good life thought Bertie, looking across at the motor-car restored to usefulness. He hoped he might never leave this absorbing occupation. It would be a sad day for him if his father decided that he should take over the family business! No – motor-cars were his own choice!

He brushed the crumbs from his clothes, stood up, and decided to visit the 'Beetle and Wedge' for a drink, before returning to Caxley.

It was a relief to the young man when Bender spoke of his affairs that evening, and he said so.

'I haven't liked to question you, Father, but I guessed things were getting more and more difficult. That business of Bob's seems to have put the lid on it.'

'Well, he's safely inside for twelve months,' replied Bender, 'and we're all a sight better off without the rascal. But North's will have to go, as far as I can see, and perhaps it's as well. I shall still be able to work here, and not have the responsibility. I tell you frankly, Bertie, I shouldn't like to go through the last year or so again.'

'You'll miss the garden,' said Bertie, looking out at the wet evening.

'There'll be another on the hill,' said Bender robustly. 'And I'm glad for your mother's sake we're making the move. It means a lot to her.'

He clapped his son on the shoulder in a dismissive way.

'Glad to have told you, Bertie. You've taken it very well. There's times I've felt I've let you all down. This used to be a real warm business, as you know. I've been a bit of a bungler, it seems to me.'

'You can put that idea out of your head,' replied Bertie. 'It's just the way things have fallen out. I, for one, won't miss the business. My heart's never been in it, as you well know.'

He made his way up to his room to change. His spirits rose as he mounted the stairs, for he was going to the Howards' and would spend the evening in Kathy's company.

He stood at the window looking down upon the glistening market square, and, for the first time since hearing the news, he felt a sudden pang.

This he would miss. He had not realized quite how much it meant to him. He could not imagine living in another house which did not look upon the market square. This scene had been the background to his entire life. He could remember being held in Vera's arms, clad in his scratchy flannel nightshirt, to watch the pigeons wheeling across the striped awnings of the market stalls. He had stood at that window in tears of fury after being banished from below for some misdemeanour. He had stood there, in quiet contemplation, soothed by the familiar shapes of the clustered buildings and the comings and goings of well-known Caxley folk. His fears and doubts, his hopes and joys, had been experienced here in the market square. Here were his roots, here was his entire past. How would he live without the market place around him, its sights and sounds, and its bustle of people?

He looked across at Howard's bakery. How could he live so far from Kathy? The thought was insupportable. He flung away from the window and tore off his working jacket in near panic. Then he recovered his control.

He was behaving like a child. He would still be living in Caxley. Kathy would still be there, lovely and loving. Who knows? One day he might come back to live in the market square, in a house of his own, with Kathy to share it.

The news that the North family was leaving the market place came as a great shock to Caxley. The business had been there for three generations, and Bender was popular. It was sad to think of that vast figure filling a doorway no longer his own. A few self-righteous and mean-spirited citizens announced that Bender had brought this humiliation upon himself by slackness and indolence. But Bender's friends rose to his support, and cried them down.

The move was a leisurely one, much to Hilda's exasperation. She would have liked to pack up and go immediately, once the decision was made, but it was not to be. Tenby's had much to arrange with Bender, and Hilda had to content herself with daily trips up the hill to supervise the painting and decorating which went on in the red-brick villa so soon to be the family home.

As usual, on these occasions, nothing in the old house seemed to fit the new one. The curtains and carpets were either too small, too large, or too shabby. Hilda nobly did her best to keep expenses down, knowing now the truth of their financial circumstances, but she fought a losing battle. Colours clashed, walnut warred with oak, the vast mahogany dining table had to be left behind because it would not go through any door or window, and a new one bought. New chintz covers became a necessity, shrouding odd chairs in a more pleasing harmony. Two fireplaces had to be replaced, and it was deemed necessary to overhaul the gas system from the attics to the cellars. Bender began to wonder if the tidy sum from Tenby's would be enough to cover the cost of the new villa, let alone leaving him a nest egg in the bank.

His own time was occupied in clearing out the main part of the premises for Tenby's agricultural equipment. A mammoth sale of kitchen hardware took place and was long remembered in Caxley in the years to come. Many a stout bread crock or set of saucepans became known in cottage homes in the Caxley district as 'one of North's last bargains'.

Most of Tenby's men were local fellows, well known to Bender, and he found no difficulty in getting on with them in the weeks that followed. Tenby himself he disliked. He was a shrewd business man, originally from the north, and thought far more quickly than Bender ever could. His beady dark eyes ran over the possibilities of the old house, and

Bender could not help feeling a qualm when he heard him discussing the advantages of ripping out the first floor walls to make one large showroom above the shop. His grey and white striped drawing-room, now standing empty, seemed to breathe a mute appeal. Where now were the red velvet chairs, the wall brackets bearing sea-lavender, and all the other familiar furnishings of his best-loved room? Bender had to admit that the new house gave him small satisfaction compared with the spacious shabby comfort of the old premises. It would be sad to see the place so altered.

It made him sadder still when he discovered that later on the firm proposed to flatten his beautiful little garden, cement it over, and to erect an enormous structure on the site to house new tractors and other large pieces of equipment. Bender could hardly bear to think about it. The pinks bordering the river bank were particularly fine in the summer of 1914, and their heady fragrance held a doomed poignancy which Bender never forgot. What had he done when he had parted with his heritage? Was it all to be destroyed?

The family was now installed on the hill. The new house was called 'Rose Lodge' which Hilda felt was refined. It took Bender years before he could write it automatically at the head of his rare letters. Somehow he always put *15 The Market Square*, before remembering the change of address.

The top two floors of the old premises were to be refurbished, 'for future staff use', as Jack Tenby said. Meanwhile, they stood empty. Sometimes Bender climbed the stairs and had a look at the bare dusty rooms. Against the walls were marks where furniture had stood for years. Here the paper had peeled where young Mary's prying fingers had been busy through the bars of her cot. There was the pale circle on the wall where Winnie's mirror had hung. And there on the corner pane were Bertie's initials, cut with his mother's diamond ring. That little escapade had earned the young ten-year-old a severe spanking, Bender recalled.

There was something infinitely pathetic in the ghostly rooms. They were full of memories. Every creak of the floor-boards, every rattle of the windows, was familiar to Bender. He had not realized how tightly the old house had entwined them all, until he had cut the bonds, only to find himself still imprisoned in memories. He threw himself into the work of supervising the changes in the shop, glad to be able to forget the silence above in the hubbub of activity below.

It was not easy, as Bender discovered, as the summer slipped by. For one thing, it was excessively hot. The market place basked in one golden day after another. The Cax seemed the only cool spot in the town, and was besieged by boys and girls swimming and paddling in the evenings. For a man of Bender's weight, the weather seemed torrid, however much the younger ones might revel in it. He took to slipping out into the doomed garden to enjoy the air and to gain refreshment from the sight of the cool water rippling by. But again the pleasure was tempered by the oppressive knowledge that this might well be the last summer in which the garden would enchant him.

It was towards the end of July that the first blow came. Bender's managership had been tacitly understood, and for three months now he had done his best to get things working smoothly, under the eye of Jack Tenby, and one or two other directors of the firm, who called in from time to time to see how things were shaping.

One morning, Bender found a letter waiting for him at the office, and he read it with mounting indignation. It said that the firm had now had a chance to make plans and were reorganizing their business, both in Caxley and elsewhere. Their young Mr Parker, of Trowbridge, who had been with the firm since leaving school, would be transferred to the agricultural department of the Caxley firm and would take up residence on the premises as soon as possible. He would be in charge of the department, and they felt sure that Mr North would give him all the cooperation he had so readily shown to the firm in the last few months. They would be pleased to maintain Mr North's present rate of pay, and hoped to have the advantage of his experience for many years to come. They were 'his faithfully'.

'Faithfully!' snorted Bender, in the privacy of the shop parlour. Was this faith? Was this trust? Was it plain honesty? The truth was that it was a dam' dirty trick, to foist a young man over him in his own shop.

'His own shop.' The words echoed in his ears. Oh, the misery of it all, thought Bender! He ground one gigantic fist into the palm of the other hand, as he read the letter anew.

This was treachery. He would have it out with Jack Tenby. They should not treat Bender North like this. For two pins he would chuck the job in and let them muddle on without his help! That would show them!

But would it! Is that what they wanted? Was he simply a nuisance to be got rid of? And if he threw up this job, where would he get another? There was the family to consider. The new house was still running away with the money at an alarming rate. Dammit all, Bender groaned, ramming the letter back into its envelope, he must try and face the stark and unpleasant fact that he was no longer his own master. It was a bitter pill to swallow at any age. At forty-eight, it was doubly bitter, Bender mourned.

All that day, Bender went mechanically about his affairs in a daze. He decided not to mention the matter to Hilda until his mind was calmer. He felt that he could not bear Hilda's protestations on his behalf, her hurt pride and her ready tears. It was a day or two later, that the second unpleasant happening occurred.

Bender was adding up figures in the shop parlour with the door open into the shop. Near by, Miss Taggerty, and another woman assistant, Miss Chapman, dusted shelves and gossiped together, imagining that they were unheard.

Miss Taggerty, still faithful to the imprisoned Bob, was as plain as ever. The increasing years and private grief had speckled her sandy hair with grey, but had not added discretion to her virtues. She rattled on, blissfully unconscious of Bender's presence so close at hand, telling of scandals past and present. Bender, used to this sort of thing, let it flow over him, until a familiar name caught his attention.

'Of course it's Les Howard's! Why should the girl say it is if it isn't? A lovely boy, old Ma Tucker told my pa. Weighed nigh on ten pounds at birth, and the spitting image of Leslie – same dark eyes and all.'

'But it might be her husband's surely?' objected Miss Chapman. 'He's dark too.'

'Not *this* dark!' pronounced Miss Taggerty triumphantly. 'And it's common knowledge that Les Howard spends far too much time there on the rounds. It's pretty lonely up Bent way. I bet she was glad of a bit of company.'

'But there's not another house in sight!' protested Miss Chapman. 'How do people know Les Howard went in?'

'There's such people as hedgers-and-ditchers, and ploughmen, and the like,' retorted Miss Taggerty. 'And they've got eyes in their heads, and wasn't born yesterday, for that matter. Besides, as I told you, the girl swears it's Leslie's and the husband swears he's going to take him to court over it.'

Bender felt it was time he made his presence known. He dropped a heavy ledger on the floor, swore, and picked it up. The clear voices stopped abruptly, to be replaced by some agitated whispering, and a muffled giggle. He heard no more of the matter, but he thought about it a great deal. If this were true, then it was time his Winnie dropped the young man pretty quickly.

In the next two days he heard the same rumour from other sources. There seemed to be some foundation for the story, and Bender's worries increased. He had half a mind to have a word with Sep about the matter, but decided to let the matter rest for a few days until he was surer of his facts.

As it happened, things came to a head precipitately within the next day or two. Although Winnie and Leslie sought each other's company still, Bender had fancied that they had seen rather less of each other since the move, and hoped that the affair might be dying a natural death. Winnie was extra busy these days at the local hospital where she was doing very well as a nurse. Her free time was scarce, and quite often she spent it lying on her bed to rest her aching legs, in the unusually hot weather.

It was now August, and as close as ever. Hilda and Bender sat in their new drawing-room with all the windows open. A pale yellow moth fluttered round the gas bracket, its wings tap-tapping on the glass globe. Bender found the noise distracting.

He was still mightily aggravated by the letter from Tenby's, and had come to realize that he was in no position to protest. Naturally, this added to his fury. He wondered, as he listened to the moth and turned the newspaper in his hands, if this were the right time to tell Hilda what had occurred. She would have to know some time about 'our young Mr Parker from Trowbridge'.

At the memory, Bender grew hotter than ever. The room seemed stifling. He undid the top button of his shirt, and turned his attention once more to the newspaper. He'd tell Hilda tomorrow. It was late. She might not sleep if he broke the news now.

There seemed mighty little comfort to be had in the paper, he reflected. All this trouble in Europe! Germany at war with Russia, and the ambassador recalled from Petersburg, and the Frenchies getting the wind up and looking to us for help! Not likely, thought Bender! Let them all get on with their squabbling safely on the other side of the English Channel!

It was at that moment that the door burst open and Leslie Howard and Winnie appeared, bright-eyed. Winnie ran to her mother, holding out her hands.

'Mummy, Leslie and I have got engaged! Look at my ring!'

Hilda's face grew rosy with mingled pleasure and wrath. What could be said in the face of such combined triumph and joy? Hilda, tears in her eyes, looked at Bender for assistance.

Something seemed to burst in Bender's head. The rumours flew back to buzz round him like stinging wasps. The heat, his private worries, the depressing newspaper, and his deep love for Winnie pressed upon him unbearably.

He flung the newspaper upon the floor and turned on Leslie.

'Engaged? That you're not, my boy, until I've had a word with you in private. Step across the hall, will you? No time like the present!'

He stormed past the young man, pale-faced, into the empty dining-room, leaving Winnie and her mother trembling.

Sep Howard did not hear of the unknown young Mr Parker's promotion until the day after Leslie's uncomfortable encounter with Bender. He did not hear, either, about that piece of news, from his son.

He was very perturbed on Bender's account. This was going to hurt him very much, and it might well mean that he would be very poorly off. Should he go once again, and offer any help that he could? It needed a certain amount of courage to face Bender at any time, but Sep remembered those words: 'You'd be the first I'd turn to, Sep,' and took heart.

He had heard the news from Jack Tenby himself, and so knew that there was no doubt about it. He decided to step across to the shop as it opened, and to do what he could.

A little nervous, as he always was when approaching Bender, yet glowing with the consciousness of doing the right thing, Sep entered North's shop. Bender glowered at him over his spectacles. His voice was gruffer than ever.

'Whatcher want?' he growled.

'A word with you, please,' answered Sep.

He followed Bender's broad back into the privacy of the shop parlour, and began, diffidently, without further ado.

'I've heard the news about the new manager, Bender. Jack Tenby mentioned it. It's very hard lines on you. Is there anything I can do?'

Bender wheeled to face him, face down, like a cornered bull, his eyes blazing and his breathing noisy. Sep began to step back in horror.

'Clear out!' said Bender, dangerously calm. 'That ain't the only news you've heard, I'll lay! You heard about that son of your'n and his goings-on?'

He threw his head up suddenly, and began to roar.

'I don't want no mealy-mouthed help from you, Sep Howard, and I don't want to see hair or hide of you or your dam' kids ever again! If Leslie comes crawling round our Winnie once more, I'll give him the hiding of his life. Clear off, clear out! And dam' well mind your own business!'

He flung open the door, bundled Sep outside, and slammed the door shut again in the little man's face. Two or three interested assistants peered furtively from behind shelves. Sep pulled his jacket straight, and walked past them with as much dignity as he could muster.

His legs trembled as he crossed the market square, and his

head buzzed with the echo of Bender's shouting. He must see Leslie at once and hear his side of this shocking story. Shaken though he was by the encounter, Sep felt more pity and concern for Bender than fear, and rejoiced in his own confidence.

His eldest boy, Jim, stood immersed in the newspaper at the bakery door. His hair was white with flour, his sleeves rolled up, and his white apron fluttered in the breeze from the river near by. The boy's face was excited. His eyes sparkled as he looked up from his reading.

'Well, dad, it looks as though we're ready for 'em! Les and I should be on our travels pretty soon according to this!'

He held out the paper so that Sep could read the headlines.

'Ultimatum to Germany. War at Midnight.'

Sep's face grew graver as he read.

'I never thought it would come to this,' he said in a low voice, as though speaking to himself. He looked soberly across the paper at his son.

'But it is the right thing to do,' he said slowly. 'No matter what the consequences are, a man must always do what he knows is right.'

He turned to enter, and his son turned to watch him go, a small erect figure, bearing himself with a dignity which the young man had never noticed before.

Across the square, Bender paced up and down the shop parlour, quivering with rage. The calendar caught his eye, and he stopped to tear off yesterday's date. What had he done, he asked himself, crumpling the paper in his hand? His world seemed in ruins. He had upset Hilda, and poor Winnie, and now he had thrown his old friend from him. What straits a man could find himself in! What depths of despair still lay ahead?

Automatically he bent to read the daily motto on the new

date. It said: Aug. 4, 1914 'Be strong and of a good courage'.

It was the final straw. Bender sank upon the office stool, dropped his burning head to the cold leather top of the desk, and wept.

Part Two

11. *Over by Christmas*

THE people of Caxley greeted the declaration of war against Germany with considerable jubilation and a certain measure of relief. Tension had been mounting steadily throughout the past week. Now that the die was cast, excitement seized them.

'That Kaiser's bin too big for 'is boots for time enough. 'E needs taking down a peg or two!' said Mrs Petty.

'Us'll daunt 'em!' declared a bewhiskered shepherd near by.

'Ah! He've got the Empire to reckon with now!' agreed his old crony, spitting a jet of tobacco juice upon the market place cobbles, with evident satisfaction. The air rang with congratulatory greetings. August Bank Holiday may have been upset a little by the news of war, but spirits were high everywhere.

The papers were full of cartoons depicting Belgium as a helpless maiden in the grip of a strong, brutal, and lustful conqueror. Chivalry flowered again in the hearts of Caxley men. Justice must be done. The weak must be protected, and who better to do it than the British, with all the might of a glorious Empire to support them? There was no possibility of failure. It was simply a question of rallying to a good cause, throwing down a despot, succouring the victims, and then returning to normal life, with the glow of work well done, and a reputation enhanced with valour.

If war had to be, then it was inspiring to be so resolutely on the right side. There was no doubt about this being a righteous cause. It was the free man's blow against slavery. It was even more exhilarating, at this time, for the common man to realize how wide-flung and mighty were the bonds of Empire. There was a sudden resurgence of pride in the colonies overseas. For some years now the word 'imperialism' had seemed tarnished. Kipling's jingoistic exhortations were out of fashion. But the older people in Caxley, including Sep and Bender, remembered the show of might at Queen Victoria's Golden and Diamond Jubilees in 1887 and 1897, and remembered it now, with fierce pride, and considerable comfort.

'You see,' Bender told Hilda, 'they'll come flocking from all over the world – black, brown, and every other colour! Wherever they salute the old Union Jack! The Kaiser hasn't a hope! It'll all be over by Christmas!'

It was the phrase which was heard on all sides: 'Over by Christmas!' As the troop trains poured through Caxley station on their way to the coast, the men shouted it jubilantly to the waving mothers and wives on the platform. Caxley had never seen such a movement of men before. This was the first European war in which England had taken part for generations, and the rumble of road and rail transport, as Haldane's Expeditionary Force moved rapidly towards France, was an inspiring sound. Between August 7th and 17th, in a period of blazing sunshine, it was said that over a hundred thousand men crossed the Channel. To the people of Caxley it seemed that most of them made their way southward through their reverberating market square.

A recruiting centre had been opened at the Town Hall and the queues waiting outside added to the noise and excitement. From all the surrounding villages and hamlets, from tumbledown cottages hidden a mile or more down leafy cart tracks, the young men found their way to the market square. They came on foot, on bicycles, on horseback and in carts, farm waggons, and motor-cars. One of the most splendid turn-outs came from Fairacre and Beech Green. Two coal-black cart horses, gleaming like jet, drew a great blue-painted waggon with red wheels into the market place. Harold Miller held the reins. His whip was decorated with red, white, and blue ribbons, and the brass work on the vehicle and the horses' harness shone like gold.

About a score of young men grinned and waved cheerfully as they clattered into the market square. Jesse Miller sat beside his brother, and among the sun-tanned men aboard could be seen the bright auburn head of Arnold Fletcher, fiancé of Dolly Clare of Fairacre. Bertie North, who had already added his name to the lengthy list, waved enthusiastically to his fellow-comrades from the doorway of his father's shop.

He had never known such deep and satisfying excitement before. Ever since he and the Howard boys had volunteered, life had assumed a purpose and meaning so far unknown to him. It was as though he had been asleep, waiting unconsciously for a call to action. Now it had come, vibrant and compelling, and Bertie, in company with thousands of other young men, responded eagerly.

Their womenfolk were not so ardent. Hilda was openly tearful. She had never made a secret of her great love for Bertie. He held a special place in her heart, and the thought of her eldest child being maimed or killed was insupportable. Winnie, though outwardly calm, was doubly anguished, for Leslie was involved, as well as Bertie.

Edna Howard, with two sons enlisted and Kathy worrying to leave home to nurse or to drive an ambulance, had her share of cares, but there was a child-like quality about her which rejoiced in the general excitement and the flags and uniforms, military bands and crowds, which enlivened Caxley at this time. It was Sep who went about his business white-faced and silent, suffering not only for his sons, but also because of his years, which denied him military action.

He grieved too for the rift which had parted him and Bender. The rebuff which he had received hurt him sorely. He was too sensitive to approach Bender again, and a quiet 'Good morning' had been greeted with a grunt and a glare from the ironmonger which froze poor Sep in his tracks. As things were, with everything in turmoil, it seemed best to leave matters alone and hope that time would bring them both some comfort.

The Corn Exchange had been turned into a medical centre, and the young men went straight there from the Town Hall. The Howard boys and Bertie were passed fit and swore to serve His Majesty the King, his heirs and successors, and the generals and the officers set over them, kissed the Bible solemnly, and looked with awed delight at the new shilling and the strip of paper bearing their army number, which each received.

'Do we get our uniform yet?' asked Jim hopefully.

' 'Old 'ard,' replied the sergeant, in charge of affairs. 'You ain't the only pebbles on the beach. You clear orf back to your jobs till you're wanted. You'll hear soon enough, mark my words. Now 'op it!'

Thus began the hardest part of this new adventure. Carrying on with an everyday job was galling in the extreme to these young men. But at least, they told each other, they were in. Some poor devils like Jesse Miller, for instance, had been found medically unfit.

Jesse was heart-broken.

'Flat feet and varicose veins, they said,' Jesse cried in disgust. 'I told 'em I could walk ten miles a day behind the plough without noticing it, but they'd have none of it. Makes me look a proper fool! But I'm not leaving it there. I'll try elsewhere, that I will! I'll get in by hook or by crook! If Harry goes, I go!'

He received a great deal of sympathy, as did other unfortunate volunteers who had been unsuccessful. It was Kathy who shocked everyone by stating a startling truth at this time.

'You'd think they'd be glad really. After all, I suppose lots of the others will be killed or wounded. I think *they're* the lucky ones.'

Her hearers looked at her aghast. What treason was this? Her brothers, and Bertie too, rounded on her abruptly. Had she no proper pride? Did patriotism mean nothing? Of course it was a deprivation for men like poor old Jesse Miller to be denied the glory of battle. They were amazed that she should think otherwise.

Kathy shrugged her pretty shoulders and tossed her dark head.

'It seems all topsy-turvy to me,' she replied nonchalantly. And, later, amidst the chaotic horror of a French battlefield, Bertie was to remember her words.

The sun blazed day after day throughout that golden August. The corn fields ripened early and there would be a bumper harvest. The lanes round Caxley were white with dust. The grass verges and thick hedges were powdered with the chalk raised by the unaccustomed volume of army traffic making its way southward.

It seemed unbelievable that within less than a hundred miles of Caxley, across a narrow ribbon of water, men were blasting each other to death.

Now and again in the noonday heat, which bathed the quiet downs in a shimmering haze, a shuddering rumble could be heard – the guns of distant battle. News of the retreat from Mons came through. It sounded ugly – *a retreat*. Surely, the Caxley folk told each other, the great British army should not be in *retreat*?

It was easy to explain away the unpleasantness. The army was simply moving to a better strategic position. They were luring the Kaiser's men to a sure defeat. There was nothing really to worry about. It would all be over by Christmas, they repeated.

But it was news of the retreat which resulted in action at last for the Caxley volunteers, for they were called up and sent to a training camp in Dorset at the beginning of September.

Winnie North was among those who crowded Caxley station to wave good-bye to Bertie and the Howard boys. She kissed them all in turn, but clung longer to Leslie. As the train drew away her gaze lingered upon his dwindling hand until it vanished around the great bend of the railway line. She returned, pale but calm, to Rose Lodge and her mother's tear-blotched face.

Three days later she broke some news to her father and mother.

'I'm being transferred to a naval hospital,' said Winnie abruptly. She had just come in from work, and still wore her nurse's uniform.

Her mother looked up, wide-eyed with shock. The khaki sock which she was knitting for Bertie fell neglected into her lap. Bender emerged from behind his newspaper and shot her a glance over the top of his spectacles.

'Oh, Winnie dear,' quavered Hilda, her lip trembling.

'Now, mother,' began Winnie firmly, as if speaking to a refractory patient, 'I volunteered for this as soon as war broke out, and I'm very lucky to be chosen. You must see that I can't stay behind when the boys have already gone.'

'Where is this place?' asked Bender.

Winnie told him. Bender's mouth took a truculent line.

'But that's near Bertie,' cried her mother, looking more cheerful.

'And Leslie Howard,' grunted Bender. 'It don't pull the wool over my eyes, me girl.'

'Dad,' said Winnie levelly, 'we've had all that out until

I'm sick of it. Once and for all, I am engaged to Leslie, whatever you say. That disgusting rumour you persist in believing hasn't a word of truth in it –'

'Winnie,' broke in Hilda, 'you are not to speak to your father like that. He acted for the best.'

'When I need your support,' bellowed Bender to his wife, 'I'll ask for it! She's nothing but a love-sick ass, and refuses to face facts. I never thought a daughter of mine would be such a fool – but there it is!'

There was an angry silence for a moment, broken at last by Winnie.

'I'll believe Leslie, if you don't mind,' she said in a low voice. 'And it may interest you to know that I didn't choose to go to this hospital – glad though I am, of course. I'm simply being drafted there, and probably not for long.'

'When do you have to go?' asked Hilda.

'Next Saturday,' said Winnie, 'so let's bury the hatchet for these few days and have a little peace.'

She rose from the chair, went across to her mother and kissed her forehead. Five minutes later they heard the bath running and Winnie's voice uplifted in song.

Bender sighed heavily.

'I'll never understand that girl,' he muttered. 'Blinding herself to that waster's faults! Leaving a comfortable home! Defying her parents!'

'She's in love,' replied his wife simply, picking up her knitting.

Rose Lodge seemed sadly quiet when Winnie had departed to her new duties. Mary, the youngest, attended a sedate little private school near her home, and seemed to spend her time in fraying old pieces of sheet for army dressings.

'Pity you don't learn your multiplication tables at the same time,' commented Bender. 'Strikes me that you'll know less than the marsh lot at the National School, when it comes to leaving. And a pretty penny it's costing us too!'

'Why can't I leave then?' urged Mary. 'I could help at the hospital, couldn't I? Sweeping, and that? Kathy Howard's started there as a nurse. Did you know?'

Bender looked at Hilda. Hilda turned a little pink. Since the row with Sep he had not spoken a word to any of the Howards if he could help it, but Hilda kept in touch.

'Well, I did just happen to run across Edna at the butcher's yesterday,' admitted his wife, 'and she mentioned it. I should think she'd make a good little nurse; cheerful and quick to learn. And it does mean she can live at home,' added Hilda, rather sadly, her thoughts with her distant Winnie.

Bender made no comment, but his frown deepened, and Hilda's heart sank. If only things could be as they used to be before that horrid little Mr Parker from Trowbridge took charge of their shop! If only Bender could shake off the cares which seemed to bow him down! In the old days, nothing had worried him, it seemed. She remembered their early troubles, their set-backs, the loss of their first baby, the financial struggles of their early years in business, Bob's duplicity, and a hundred other problems. Somehow Bender had always faced things cheerfully, his great laugh had blown away her cares throughout their married life, until this last disastrous year. If only he could recover his old spirits!

She made a timid suggestion, hoping to distract his mind from the Howards' affairs and turn it to happier things.

'Shall we go and have a look at the dahlias, dear?'

'No thanks,' said Bender shortly. 'Nothing seems to do as well here as in the old garden. It's disheartening.'

He slumped back into his armchair and closed his eyes. It was, thought Hilda, as if he wanted to shut out the sight of the pretty new drawing room at Rose Lodge. Was he, in spirit, perhaps, back in the old room above the shop where they had spent so many evenings together? How helpless she felt, in the face of this silent unhappiness! Would there never be an end to it?

Letters came regularly from Winnie and Bertie during the following months. They met occasionally. Both looked extraordinarily well, they assured their parents separately. Bertie had put on almost a stone in weight, and there were rumours that his unit would be off to France before Christmas. If so, there would be leave, of course. Bertie said he would let them know just as soon as he knew himself. Hilda was buoyed up with hope, and hurried about making a hundred preparations, refusing to think further than the homecoming.

Winnie mentioned Leslie in her letters, but did not speak of her feelings. Hilda guessed that she did not want to upset her father by introducing the contentious subject.

At the beginning of December two letters arrived at Rose Lodge. Bertie's said that his week's leave began on the following day, and would his mother cook a really square meal? Winnie's said that she too had leave, and would be arriving three days after Bertie. She too could do with a square meal. Singing, Hilda made her way to the kitchen to make joyful preparations. Bender, smiling at last, stumped down the hill to the shop, which he had come to loathe, to embark on the day's work with rather more eagerness than usual.

Across the market square, Sep Howard stood in the kitchen reading a letter from Leslie. He too was smiling. Edna waited anxiously for him to finish, so that she could read it for herself.

He handed it over with a happy sigh.

'Read that, my love,' he said gently.

Edna's eyes widened as she read, and her pretty mouth fell open.

'Married?' she whispered.

'Married!' repeated Sep huskily. To Edna's surprise, she saw that there were tears in his eyes. She had never realized that Leslie had meant so much to him.

But it was not Leslie, nor his bride, that occupied Sep's thoughts. This, Sep told himself thankfully, must heal the breach between Bender and himself. At last his earnest prayers had been answered.

12. *An Unwelcome Marriage*

BERTIE's homecoming was such a joyful occasion, he looked so fit and happy, that neither of his parents noticed a certain constraint in his manner. His appetite was enormous, his eagerness to visit his Caxley friends so keen, that Hilda was kept busy providing meals and entertainment.

Winnie was expected the following Wednesday.

'Did she tell you what time she would arrive?' asked Hilda at breakfast. 'I must go shopping this morning, but I don't want to be out when she comes.'

'I don't think she'll be here much before this evening,' said Bertie slowly.

'How late!' exclaimed Hilda. 'Won't she catch the same train as you?'

'I doubt it,' replied Bertie briefly, and escaped from the room.

All that day, Hilda went about her affairs, humming cheerfully. Bertie watched her carry a vase of late chrysanthemums up the stairs to Winnie's room. When darkness fell, she refused to draw the curtains in the drawing room, hoping to catch the first glimpse of Winnie coming up the path.

It was very quiet that evening. Bender dozed in his armchair, Hilda was stitching braid on a skirt, and Bertie flipped idly through the pages of the *Caxley Chronicle*. It was nearly eight o'clock when they heard the sound of footsteps on the gravel outside, and before Hilda could fold up her sewing and hurry out, the door opened and, Winnie, smiling and radiant, blinking in the unaccustomed light, stood on the threshold. Behind her was a tall figure.

'Leslie!' exclaimed Hilda involuntarily. The joy in her

face faded to a look of apprehension. The couple came into the room and Bender awoke.

'What the devil –' he rumbled truculently, eyeing the young man. Winnie went forward swiftly, kissed him, and pushed him back again into the armchair.

'Don't say anything, Dad dear, just listen,' she pleaded. She turned to face them.

'Leslie and I are married. It's no good scolding us, either of you. So, please, *please*, forgive us and say you hope we'll be happy.'

Hilda moved forward, her face working. She took Winnie in her arms and gave her a gentle kiss, but there were tears in her eyes.

'You should have told us,' she protested. 'You should have written. This hurts us all so terribly.'

Bender had struggled to his feet. His face was red, his head thrust forward like an angry bull.

'This is a fine way to treat your mother and me,' he growled thickly. 'You'll get no forgiveness from me – either of you – whatever your mother does.'

He glared round the room and caught sight of Bertie's pale face. Something in it made him start forward.

'You knew about this,' he said accusingly. Bertie nodded.

'I stood witness, Dad,' he said. 'I'm sorry.'

There was a dreadful silence, broken only by Bender's laboured heavy breathing. At last he gave a great gasp, shouldered his way blindly across the room, and burst through the French windows into the garden, leaving them to clang behind him.

'Bender!' cried Hilda, beginning to follow, but Bertie caught her arm.

'He's better alone, mamma,' he said quietly. 'Sit down, and I'll bring you a drink.'

He turned to the young couple.

'No doubt you'll need one too.' He moved a chair forward

for Winnie and motioned the silent Leslie to another. There was an authority about him which cooled the situation.

'It would have been nice to drink a toast to your future happiness,' said Bertie, when the glassess were filled, 'but this does not seem quite the time to do it.'

Hilda, trembling, took a sip and then put down her glass carefully on the work-box beside her.

'This has been such a shock – such an awful shock! You know how your father has felt, Winnie. And as for you, Leslie, I don't think we shall ever be able to forgive you. So underhand, so sly –!' She began to fumble for a handkerchief.

'Mamma, it was no use telling you anything. Neither you nor Dad would listen. We knew that. We were determined to get married. Now we have. In a registry office. You'll simply have to get used to the idea.'

Leslie spoke at last.

'I wanted to write, but Winnie felt it was far better to come and tell you ourselves when it was all over. I promise you I'll take care of her. You must know that.'

'I don't know that,' responded Hilda with a flash of spirit, 'which is why we opposed the match. But now it's done, then all I can say is that I sincerely *hope* you will take care of her.'

Practical matters now came to the front of her distracted mind. Winnie's room lay ready for her, but what should be done with Leslie? If only Bender would return from the garden! If only he would give her some support in this dreadful moment!

As though divining her thoughts Winnie spoke.

'We're not going to stay, Mamma, as things are. Father's too upset, and it will take him a little while to get used to the idea. Aunt Edna has offered us a room and we'll call here again tomorrow morning. We'll try to have a word now with Dad before we go.'

She kissed her mother again and squeezed her gently.

'Cheer up, my love. We're so happy, don't spoil it for us. And try to persuade Father that it isn't the end of the world.'

'I'm afraid it *is* the end of the world for him,' replied Hilda sadly.

The young couple made their way into the dark garden followed by Bertie.

'Dad!' called Winnie.

'Dad!' called Bertie.

But there was no reply. Bender was a mile away, walking the shadowy streets of Caxley, his mind in torment as he looked for comfort which could not be found.

Hilda, alone in the room, wept anew. 'Aunt Edna!' It was hard to bear. That Edna Howard should be the one to whom her Winnie turned in trouble was a humiliation she had never imagined.

She thought of all her own loving preparations during the day. Winnie's bed was turned down, the sheet snowy and smooth above the pink quilt. A hot water bottle lay snugly in the depths. The late chrysanthemums scented the room with their autumnal fragrance.

Winnie married! And in a registry office too! Some dim sordid little room with no beauty about it, she supposed. All her plans for Winnie's wedding had shattered before her eyes. Where now were her dreams of a blue and white wedding, white roses, lilies, and delphiniums decorating the church, and Winnie herself a vision in bridal white?

It had all been so clear, even down to Mary's blue and white bridesmaid's frock and the posy of white rosebuds with long blue ribbons streaming from it. Somehow the bridegroom had always been a shadowy figure – just someone pleasant and kind, with a good bank balance, of course, and a natural desire for a reasonably sized family, sensibly spaced for dear Winnie's sake. That anything as catastrophic as this could happen threw Hilda's world into utter chaos. How would she ever face the other Caxley matrons? And worst of all, how could she face Edna Howard?

But this was in the future. The first thing was to comfort poor Bender. He must, somehow, be made to see that the situation must be accepted, regrettable though it was. Winnie, foolish and disobedient, was still their daughter, after all.

She mopped her eyes resolutely. All that was left for them now was to be brave, and make the best of a very bad job.

But Hilda's efforts were not to begin until the next day, for Bender did not return until the small hours of the morning, long after Hilda had taken her aching head to bed. And, as she feared, when she broached the painful subject after breakfast, Bender refused to discuss it.

'Don't speak to me about it,' he said warningly. 'I've had enough at the moment. To think that Winnie's behaved like this! And that Bertie knew about it all the time! A fine pair of children! I'd expect no more from a Howard than Leslie's shown us, but that Winnie and Bertie could treat us so shabby – well, it's like being betrayed!'

Hilda's lip began to tremble and Bender began to speak more gently.

'Let me go to the shop now, there's a love. I'll work it off, maybe, and feel better when I come home. But I can't face my family – nor that dam' scoundrel Leslie – yet awhile.'

It was Bertie who made his father face him, later that day. In these last few hours Bertie seemed to have become very grown up, and might almost be the head of the house himself, thought Hilda wonderingly, watching her son shepherd Bender into the dining room for a private talk.

'I won't keep you long, father,' said Bertie, closing the door behind him, 'but I've only three or four days' leave left and I'm not having it spoilt by this affair. I'm sorry to have deceived you, but Winnie insisted, and frankly, I'd do it all over again, in the circumstances.'

'Bad enough deceiving me,' retorted Bender, 'but a sight worse to let a Howard marry your sister.'

'I think I know Leslie better than you do,' replied Bertie calmly. 'He's not the man I should have chosen for Winnie, but it's her choice, and I honestly think he loves her.'

Bender snorted derisively.

'He's ready to settle down,' continued Bertie levelly, 'and Winnie's the one to help him. Dash it all, father, we've known the Howards all our lives! How would you have felt if she had run off with a complete stranger? It's happening often enough in wartime! For your own sake, as well as Winnie's and Mamma's, do try and accept this business sensibly. It does no good to keep up a useless feud, and to make the whole family unhappy.'

'It's easy to talk!' replied Bender. 'I can't forget what I know about that young man, and I can't believe he'll treat Winnie properly.'

'All the more reason why you should stand by her now,' retorted Bertie. 'If she's in trouble she'll need her home.'

'You're right, I don't doubt, my boy,' said Bender sadly. 'I'll ponder it, but I can't see much good coming of it. I wonder what Sep and Edna think of it all?'

'They're delighted,' Bertie told him. 'Made them very welcome when they arrived, Winnie said.'

A thought struck Bender. He looked shrewdly at Bertie over his spectacles.

'They knew, did they?'

'Leslie wrote on his wedding day,' said Bertie shortly. 'He knew they'd be pleased.'

'But Winnie didn't,' murmured Bender, as if to himself.

'She knew you wouldn't be,' Bertie said simply, and left his father alone with his thoughts.

*

That evening there was a dance at the Corn Exchange. Bertie dressed with unusual care and studied his reflection in the mirror with considerable misgivings. What a very undistinguished appearance he had! He disliked his fair hair and his blue eyes. To his mind they appeared girlish. He wondered if a moustache might improve his looks. Too late to bother about that now, anyway, he told himself, looking at his watch.

The newly-weds and Jim and Kathy were to be of the party, and Bertie was relieved to leave the heavy atmosphere of Rose Lodge behind him and stride down the hill to the market square. It was a crisp clear night, full of stars. Now and again the whiff of a dying bonfire crossed his path, that most poignant of winter smells. It was good to be back in the old town. It was better still to be on the way to meeting Kathy. Tonight he would ask her.

The Corn Exchange was gay with the flags of all nations. Ragtime music shook the hall, and there was an air of determined hilarity about the many dancers, as though, for this evening, at least, they would forget the horrors of war, and simply remember that music and rhythm, youth and excitement, also had a place in the scheme of things.

Leslie and Winnie danced together, heads close, oblivious to all about them. They had always danced well together, thought Bertie, gazing at them over the dark hair of Kathy, his own partner. They looked happy enough, in all conscience. If only he could quell the little nagging doubt at the back of his own mind! He looked into Kathy's eyes and forgot his sister's affairs.

It was agony to part from her and to watch other partners claim her. Kathy's dance programme was much too full for Bertie's liking. There was no one else in the room that he wanted to partner, but Caxley eyes were as sharp as ever, and he dutifully piloted a few young ladies about the floor, his eyes on Kathy the while. She was lovelier than ever –

vivacious, sparkling, light as a feather. Had he any hope at all, wondered Bertie, stumbling over his partner's foot and apologizing abstractedly?

She was dancing with one of the Crockford boys. How unnecessarily damned handsome they were, thought Bertie crossly! When the Crockfords were not large and red-headed, they were tall, elegant and dark. This one had hair oiled till it shone like jet, a handsome black moustache, and an enviable turn of speed when he reversed. Kathy was gazing at him in a way that Bertie found infuriating. As soon as the dance was over he hurried to her side.

'Come outside for a moment,' he begged.

'Why?' asked Kathy. Her bright eyes darted everywhere about the hall. Her little satin slipper tapped the floor in time to the music. *'Hullo! Hullo! Who's your lady friend?'* throbbed through the hall, and the refrain was taken up by many voices. The noise was unbearable to Bertie.

'It's quieter,' he shouted, above the din. Kathy rose rather reluctantly, and followed him outside into the market place. It was deliciously fresh and cool after the stuffiness of the Corn Exchange, but Kathy shivered and pulled her silk shawl round her.

'Let's go and look at the river,' said Bertie.

'We'll miss the dancing.'

'Only this one,' promised Bertie. He put his arm through hers and led her past her own house and down the narrow lane leading to the tow path. The noise behind them died away. Only the plop of a fish and the quiet rippling of the Cax disturbed the silence. They made their way to the little bridge and leant over. Now that Bertie had succeeded in bringing Kathy here, he became horribly nervous. So much depended on the next few minutes. He took a deep breath and began.

'Kathy, I've wanted to ask you often. You must know how I feel about you. Do you care about me at all?'

'Of course I do,' said Kathy, with a cheerful promptness that made Bertie despair. 'I care very much about you. And Leslie and Jim, and all my friends who are fighting.'

Bertie sighed and took her hand. It was small and thin, and very cold.

'Not that way, Kathy. I meant, do you love me? I love you very much, you know. Enough to marry you. Could you ever think about that?'

Kathy laughed and withdrew her hand. It fluttered to Bertie's hot cheek and patted it affectionately.

'Oh, Bertie dear, don't talk so solemnly! I'm not thinking of marrying for years yet! Not you – or anyone else! There's too much fun to be had first! Take me back, Bertie, it's cold, and I want to dance.'

He tried once more, putting his arms round her, and tilting up her chin so that he could look into her lovely face.

'Please, Kathy,' he entreated, 'think about it. I know you're young, but I love you so much. Say you'll think about it!'

She pushed him away pettishly.

'I'm not going to promise any such thing. I want to be free, and you ought to be too!' She took his arm again and began to pull him back towards the market square.

'Come on, Bertie, I shall miss the next dance and it's a military two-step. Don't be stuffy, there's a love. You're a dear old stick really!'

They walked back to the Corn Exchange, Bertie in silence, Kathy chattering of he knew not what. At the doorway he stopped.

'I won't come in,' he said. 'I've a headache. Go and enjoy yourself.'

She tripped in without once looking back, arms outstretched to her waiting partner.

Bertie turned away, and made his way blindly to the drinking fountain in the middle of the square. He filled one of the iron cups and drank the icy water. The feel of the cold iron chain running through his hot palm reminded him of the times he had sought refreshment here as a boy.

He leant his head against the comforting cold plinth beneath the Queen's bronze skirts, and looked across the square towards his old house. If only he could turn back the years! If only he could be a boy again, with none of a man's troubles to torture him!

It was almost a relief to return to his unit. The prospect of going overseas was one to look forward to after the unhappy events of this disastrous leave. He was glad to let other people make the decisions for him. Whatever the future held could give Bertie no more pain, he felt sure, than the grief of his family and the bitter disappointment of Kathy's complete disregard of his feelings.

In the crowded railway carriage rattling to Dorset through the darkening winter afternoon, Bertie re-lived again those moments with Kathy. To be called a 'dear old stick!' He shuddered at the remembrance. What hope was there ever for him, if those were her feelings? He remembered his last glimpse of her at Caxley Station. To his surprise she had come to see off the three of them, for Winnie and Leslie too were on the train.

She had kissed them all in turn. He felt her kisses still upon his cheek, as cold and light as moths, and his heart turned over. One thing he knew, whatever happened to him here, or in France, now or in the future, there would be nobody else for him but Kathy. Always, and only, Kathy.

He closed his eyes. The train roared through a cutting, carrying him unprotesting to whatever the future might hold.

13. Caxley at War

THE bells of St Peter's rang out across the market square and the rosy roofs of Caxley on Christmas morning. Bender, Hilda, and Mary hurried up the steps and made their way to their usual pew.

The church was unusually full. Across the aisle the Crockford family filled two pews. They must have a houseful for Christmas, thought Hilda, with a pang of envy. Dan was making one of his rare appearances in church, his leonine head glowing against the murky shadows of the old building.

As the organ played the voluntary, Hilda gazed up the long nave and let her sad thoughts wander. If only Bertie and Winnie were here! But Bertie and the Howard boys and the rest of their company were somewhere in France, and Winnie was still nursing at the hospital in Dorset.

If only Winnie could have chosen someone else to marry! What a wedding Hilda had planned for her, with this noble church as its setting! She could see it so clearly in her mind's eye – the lilies on the altar, where now the Christmas roses and the scarlet-berried holly glowed, the smilax and white rosebuds where now the glossy ivy trailed its dark beauty. And there, at the altar, her dear Winnie in the beautiful wedding gown with the long train which she had so often visualized!

Tears blurred Hilda's eyes. The nave and chancel swam mistily before her, and she was glad to hear the gentle meanderings of the organist turn to the loud joyful strains of 'Adeste Fideles' as the choir entered, singing, and the congregation rose to join in praise.

'Please, God,' prayed Hilda desperately, as she struggled

to her feet, 'let us all be together next Christmas, and let us all be happy again!'

Not far away, Edna Howard, beside Sep in the chilly chapel, wondered too about her two children in a foreign land. To think that this time last year she was positively looking forward to 1914! It had brought nothing but trouble!

The minister's voice droned on, but Edna did not attend to his exhortations. Sometimes she doubted if there were really any God to speak to. Sep said there was, and seemed to be comforted by the knowledge, and Edna had never expressed any of her own doubts. It would have upset Sep so much. But when you heard of the terrible things that the Germans were doing, then surely there couldn't be a God or he would never let it happen?

Edna mused vaguely on her uncomfortable bench, until her attention was caught by a white thread on the sleeve of her coat. She plucked it away neatly, let it flutter to the scrubbed floor boards so near her painful knees, and stroked the fur of her cuffs lovingly. It was wearing very well, she thought. After all, she had had it a whole year now, and it still looked as good as new. How kind Sep was to her! She stole a glance at his pale face beside her. His eyes were shut fast, his dark lashes making little crescents. His lips were pressed together with the intensity of his concentration. He was in communion with his Maker, and for Sep the world had ceased to exist.

Perhaps, thought Edna, returning to the contemplation of her coat, it could be turned in a few years' time. It was good stuff ...

It was during the next week that Hilda heard how Bertie had spent his Christmas Day in the front line somewhere south of Armentières. His letter read:

Dearest Mamma,

I opened your parcel on Christmas morning and everything in it was first-class. Thank you all very much. The cake was shared with some of the other Caxley chaps who appreciated it very much.

The queerest thing happened here. Just before dawn we heard the Germans in their trench opposite singing carols. They sang 'Peaceful Night, Holy Night' – only in German, of course, and we joined in. After a bit, one of our officers went into no-man's-land and met one of theirs, and gradually we all climbed out and wished each other 'Happy Christmas' and exchanged cigarettes. Some were from your parcel, mamma, and I hope you don't mind a few of them going to the enemy. I can assure you, they did not seem like enemies on Christmas morning. We kept the truce up long enough to bring in our dead.

Further down the line, we heard, both sides had a game of football together. It makes you realize what a farce war is – nobody wants it. But it looks as though it will drag on for a long time yet, I'm afraid.

My love to you and to all the family,

Your loving son,
Bertie

Bertie's fears were echoed by all at home. The cheerful cry: 'Over by Christmas' was heard no more. Fighting was going on in all parts of the world, and the news from the western front grew grimmer weekly. It was here that the local men were engaged, and anxious eyes read the columns of 'Dead, Wounded, and Missing' which were published regularly in the *Caxley Chronicle*. It was a sad New Year for many families in Caxley, as 1915 came in, and the knowledge that losses must continue to be very heavy was too terrible to contemplate.

For Bender, at least, the war had brought one small consolation. He was again in charge of the old shop, and all alterations had been postponed. Young Mr Parker was serving in the Navy, one or two of the assistants had also gone to the war and Bender struggled on with Miss Taggerty and a chuckle-headed boy from Springbourne, called Ralph Pringle, as his only support.

It suited Bender. Trade was slack, so that he was not overworked, and he had time to look after the shabby empty rooms of his late home, and to keep the beloved garden tidy. It was a reprieve for North's, Bender thought, and he was thankful.

He had recovered some of his old zest, doing his best to cheer Hilda now that Bertie was away from home. They spoke little of the disastrous marriage. The subject was too painful, but time and the background of war did much to lessen the tension. Hilda held weekly sewing parties in her new drawing room and busied herself in packing up the results to be sent to the Front.

Bender joined the local branch of the Home Defence Corps and thoroughly enjoyed his evenings at the Corn Exchange or in the Market Square. He, in company with other Caxley men too old for military service, drilled rigorously. Stiff joints and creaking knee-caps gave off reports as loud as the guns they longed to have, and although they knew in their hearts that their contribution was pitifully inadequate, yet they enjoyed the comradeship, the exercise, and the feeling of being alert.

Sep Howard was not among them. He had joined the Red Cross at the outbreak of war, and spent many nights at Caxley Station tending the wounded on their way to hospital from the battle front. He never forgot those tragic hours.

Between trains, Caxley station lay dim and quiet in the hollow by the river. The waiting room had been turned into a canteen. Urns bubbled, sandwiches were stacked and the helpers' tongues were as busy as their willing hands. Sometimes Sep left the warm fugginess to pace the deserted dark platform. Alone under the stars he walked up and down, watching the gleam of rails vanishing into the distance, and listening for the rumble of the next train bearing its load of broken men. His compassion had quickly overcome the physical nausea which blood and vomit inevitably aroused. He had become used to limbs frighteningly awry, to empty sleeves, and to heads so muffled in cotton wool and bandages that nothing emerged from them but screams.

Sep was recognized as one of the most tireless workers, with an uncanny gift of easing pain.

'I'm used to working at night,' he said simply, 'and I try to move the chaps the way my mother handled me when I was ill. She was a good nurse.'

He gained great satisfaction from the voluntary work. He recoiled from the martial side of war and even more from the pomp and glory of its trappings. Military bands, flags fluttering, soldiers in splendid array, all gave Sep a cold sickness in his heart. He had viewed with tears the jubilant crowd outside the Town Hall at the outbreak of war. The boisterous zeal of the elderly Home Defence Corps was not to Sep's liking. He found himself nearer the truth of war in those dark pain-filled hours at Caxley station.

He had seen Bender stepping out bravely with his fellows as they marched through the streets of Caxley to some military exercise on one of the surrounding commons. After the terrible scene in Bender's office, Sep had purposely kept out of his way, but had longed for things to be easier between them.

He had never been able to find out the truth about the ugly rumour of the girl at Bent. Leslie had denied the whole thing roundly when he had asked him about the matter. Sep was still troubled about the affair, and could not wholly believe his son, but was too proud to do more than accept Leslie's word. In any case, both he and Edna were delighted with his marriage to Winnie, and welcomed the couple whenever they could manage a brief visit. One must look forward, not back, Sep told himself.

As the early weeks of 1915 passed, Sep was relieved to see Bender looking more cheerful. Now they spoke when they met. Topics were kept general, inquiries were made about each other's families, but no mention was ever made of Winnie and Leslie between the two men. There was still a constraint about each meeting, but at least the ice was broken, and Sep hoped earnestly that one day he and Bender would be completely at ease with each other. The families did not meet so readily these days. Since the move, and since the war began, they had grown apart. The younger children did not mix as readily as the older ones had done when they lived so near each other in the market place, and the marriage had proved another barrier, much to Sep's grief.

It was in February that the Howard family had its first blow. Two local men had been killed near the Ypres Canal, and one of them was Jim Howard. The other was Arnold Fletcher, the gardener at Beech Green, and the fiancé of Dolly Clare who taught at Fairacre.

Sep received the news with numbed dignity, Edna with torrents of tears and furious lamentations. Sep grieved for her, but secretly envied the ease of her outbursts, for they were so exhausting that she slept soundly at nights. He went about his affairs pale and silent, and refused to give up his Red Cross vigils, even on the night of the news. Each man that he tended was Jim to him, and from this he gained strength.

Bender heard the news as the wintry sun was setting behind St Peter's. Without a word he made his way across the square, still clad in his shop overall, and went into the bakehouse in the yard. As he had suspected, Sep was there alone, stacking tins automatically, his face stricken.

'Sep,' muttered Bender, putting one massive hand on each

side of Sep's thin shoulders and gazing down at him. 'What can I say?'

Sep shook his head dolefully. He did not trust himself to speak.

'I feel it very much,' went on Bender gruffly. 'And so will Hilda. We were always very fond of your Jim – a fine boy.'

Sep bit his quivering lip but remained silent. Bender dropped his hands and sat down heavily on the great scrubbed table, sighing gustily.

'This bloody war,' he growled, 'is going to cause more heartache than we reckoned, Sep. Who'd have thought, when our kids were playing round the old Queen out there, that it would have come to this?'

He gazed unseeingly at the brick floor and his two great black boots set upon it. After a minute's silence he shook himself back into the present, and began to make his way to the door. It was then that Sep found his voice.

'It was good of you to come, Bender. I've missed you.'

'Well, we've had our ups and downs, Sep,' replied Bender, turning in the doorway, 'and there's some things we'll never see eye to eye about. But in times like this we forget 'em.'

His voice dropped suddenly.

'God's truth, Sep, I'm sorry about this. I'm sorry for all of us with sons these days.'

And before Sep could reply he had turned the corner and vanished.

The war dragged on. Food was getting short, and the posters everywhere exhorted men and women to save every crumb and to guard against waste. Caxley did not feel the want of food as harshly as the larger towns. Set amidst countryside, with the Cax meandering through it, vegetables, fruit, eggs, milk, and river fish were comparatively easy to come by. There was a shortage of sugar, and sweets, and Mary North was told never to ask for such things when they were visiting.

'People haven't enough for themselves,' pointed out Hilda. 'Just say you aren't very hungry.'

'But I'm *always* hungry for sweets,' protested Mary. 'You wouldn't want me to lie?'

'There are such things as *white* lies!' responded Hilda. 'And in wartime you'll have to make use of them.'

Certainly there were minor hardships as well as the dreadful losses overseas which cast their shadows. But the spirit of the people was high, and many of the women were tasting independence for the first time. They set off daily to munitions factories or shops, enjoying company and the heady pleasure of earning money of their own. They did not intend to throw this freedom away when the war ended. As they worked they talked and laughed, as they had never done cooped up in their own homes, and snippets of news about local fighting men were always the first to be exchanged. So often they were sad items, but now and again there was good news, and there was great excitement in 1916 when Caxley heard that Harold Miller had been commissioned at Thiepval after displaying great gallantry. His brother, Jesse, still struggling with the farm and with very little help, received many congratulations on market day that week.

It was towards the end of the same year that Hilda had a letter from Winnie to say that a baby was expected the next summer. She sounded happy and well. She was living in a small flat near the hospital, where she was going to remain at work for as long as possible. There were also plans for her to have the baby there in a small maternity wing attached to the main hospital.

Leslie was still in France and had taken to army life very well. He made a good soldier, quick, obedient, and cheerful, and had received his commission about the same time as Harold Miller. He did not write to Winnie as often as she would have liked, but as things were, she readily forgave him. Now that the baby was coming, she longed for the war to end, so that they could settle down together as a family.

Hilda was delighted with the news and even Bender softened at the idea of a grandchild in the family. The Howards were even more pleased, but Sep had the sense to resist mentioning it when he and Bender met. Let him make the first move, thought Sep!

One wet November day when the market square was lashed with rain and the wet leaves fluttered about the garden of Rose Lodge, the postman arrived at the North's door with another letter.

Bender took it in and tore it open. His face grew pale as he read the message and he put a hand on the door for support.

Hilda came up the hall to him, perplexed. He handed her the flimsy paper in silence.

Trembling, Hilda read it aloud.

'We regret to inform you that your son has been wounded and is receiving medical attention at the above military hospital. He may be visited at any time.'

Wonderingly she raised her face and looked at her husband. His expression was grim and determined.

'Put on your coat, my dear. We'll go at once.'

14. Caxley Greets the Armistice

THE hospital lay a little way from Bath, some sixty miles or so from Caxley. Bill Blake, who owned the motor firm where Bertie worked in peace time, drove them there himself.

There was little talking on the journey. Hilda gazed through the rain-spattered windscreen at the wind-blown countryside. The sky was grey and hopeless, the trees bowed, the grass flattened. Long puddles lined the road reflecting the dull skies above. They passed little on the long agonizing journey, except an occasional army lorry which only reminded them more sharply of their purpose.

In happier days the hospital was a country mansion. The three mounted the long flight of steps, dreading what lay ahead. Within a few minutes, formalities were over and they found themselves at Bertie's bedside. He was barely conscious and very pale, but he smiled when he saw them.

They had been told that one leg was badly shattered and that a bullet had gone clean through his upper arm. Loss of blood was the chief cause for concern. He had lain for several hours in the mud before he had reached a field station.

Bender never forgot Hilda's bravery at that time. Not a tear fell. She smiled as encouragingly at her son as she had done years before when he was bed-bound by some childish ailment.

'You'll be home again soon, my dear,' she whispered to him, as she kissed his waxen face gently. 'Back safely in Caxley, you remember?'

He nodded very slightly, his blue eyes bemused. She could not know that the word 'Caxley' brought back a vision of the market square to him, framed in the familiar curtains of his old Caxley bedroom.

They were only allowed to stay for two or three minutes before being ushered out by the nurse.

'The doctor thinks he will be able to operate tomorrow or the next day,' the sister told them later. 'Of course he's gravely ill, but he's a strong young man and all should go well, we hope.'

With this guarded encouragement to give them cold comfort, the three made their farewells, and returned sadly along the road to Caxley.

The hours seemed endless when they reached home, and there was little sleep for Hilda and Bender in the next two nights. Bender rang the hospital twice a day, and at last he spoke to the surgeon who had operated that afternoon.

'He's doing fine,' said the voice, warm and hearty at the other end of the line. 'The arm should be as good as new in a few weeks. Just a little stiffness maybe.'

'And the leg?' Bender pressed the receiver closer to his ear. Hilda stood beside him and he clasped her hand with his free one. She could only hear the distant murmur of the surgeon's voice, but her eyes scanned Bender's face anxiously. His grip tightened, he swallowed noisily, and his voice was husky when he said the final words.

'I'm sure you did. Quite sure you did. It's a sore blow, but you know we're grateful to you. Good-bye.'

He hung up and turned to his wife.

'The leg is not as bad as they feared, but his foot, Hilda ... His foot has had to come off ...'

Bender had expected tears, but they did not come. For all her pallor, Hilda looked calm.

'I'm thankful,' she said in a low tone. 'Honestly thankful! Now he'll never have to go back. He'll be safe at home for always.'

Women, thought Bender in wonderment, were truly unpredictable.

Bertie's lengthy convalescence took place at a riverside nursing home within fifteen miles of Caxley. He made slow but steady progress, but endured great pain, and had to learn to walk again with an artificial foot.

Lying in bed, or in a chair on the green lawn sloping down to the river, he had plenty of time for thought. In many ways he regretted the end of his soldiering days, but he was realistic enough to be grateful that he need not return to active fighting. He had seen enough of war's squalor and agony to sicken him, and had often remembered Kathy's remarks about 'the lucky ones who were left at home'. He did not think she was wholly right, but he could see her point more clearly now.

But what of the future? Bill Blake had guaranteed him a job in the firm – possibly a partnership after the war. He looked forward to returning. There was no place like Caxley and no business like the motor business. It should be more flourishing than ever when the war ended. He supposed he would live at Rose Lodge as before, but he longed to have a place of his own. If only he could have gone back to the old home!

He thought, as he so often did, of Kathy. He had never met another girl to touch her, and felt positive that he never would. But how could he ask any girl to marry such an old crock? He was irritable when he was in pain, which was most of the time, and devilish slow in making progress with the new foot. He must simply persevere and hope that things grew easier. Meanwhile, he received many Caxley friends, and learnt all he could about Kathy's circumstances. She was still nursing at Caxley Hospital, he heard, and having as gay a time as war allowed in the evenings.

Bill Blake, who knew what was in Bertie's mind without

being told, offered to bring Kathy over one afternoon when she was free, and was as good as his word.

Bertie watched the clock anxiously all the morning. By two o'clock when she was due, he was in a state of feverish excitement. He sat in a wicker chair on the lawn waiting impatiently.

She was as lovely as ever when she finally arrived, clad in a pink fluttery frock with pearls at her throat. Her dark hair was piled on top, her great eyes danced as gaily as ever. She gave him a light kiss, making his head swim, and settled herself in a chair beside him. Bill, the soul of tact, vanished to make some imaginary adjustment to the car which had brought them.

They fell into conversation as easily as ever. Kathy told Bertie all about her life at the hospital. She chattered of the patients, the staff, the doctors. She talked of the Howards and the fun of looking forward to being aunt to Leslie's baby. Only when she spoke of Jim did her lovely face cloud over, and she let Bertie take her hand. But within a minute she was happy again, and Bertie thought how like her mother she was, with the same gaiety and the same ability to throw off trouble. Could it be lack of feeling? Sadly, listening to the welcome prattling, Bertie realized that it could, but he would not have her any different. Kathy was perfect.

'Want to see me walk?' asked Bertie suddenly. Kathy leapt to her feet. They made careful progress along a path beside the river.

'It reminds me of the Cax,' said Bertie, shading his eyes with his hand and gazing along the shining water. 'It makes me think of you. I still do you know.'

Kathy squeezed his arm, her smile mischievous.

'Bertie, don't think of me any more. I wasn't going to say anything. Nobody knows – not a soul. But I'm going to tell you, because somehow I can tell you everything. I'm going to be engaged any day now. We shall tell our families this week.'

It was as well that Kathy's arm supported him for Bertie could have fallen with the shock. It was really no great surprise. He had known that Kathy must marry one day and that his own case was now doubly hopeless. She had never felt for him in that way, and now his injuries made him shy of asking her again. But now that the blow had fallen it was hard to bear.

'Say you're pleased, Bertie dear. I shall be so miserable if you're not pleased. I'm very fond of you. I want you to like Henry. Shall I bring him next time?'

Bertie did his best to rally. She was gazing at him anxiously for his approval. He could deny her nothing, and told her sincerely that he hoped she would always be happy. The unknown Henry he loathed with all his being at the moment, but supposed he would feel less savage when he got used to the idea. But God help him if he was not good to Kathy!

He let Kathy tell him more, glad to be silent to regain his composure. Henry was very tall, and big, with red hair. He was in a Scottish regiment. (That damned kilt, groaned Anglo-Saxon Bertie inwardly! What havoc it caused among susceptible young women!) He was as brave as a lion, and always happy. (Who wouldn't be with Kathy beside him, thought poor Bertie?) His home was in Edinburgh and he had shown her pictures of the great castle there. He would take her to see it, on his next leave, and then she would stay with his parents. They hoped to marry in the spring.

It was small wonder that Bill Blake thought Bertie looked a bit off colour when he returned to take tea on the lawn. He commented on it with some concern, adding that there were bound to be ups and downs in a long illness.

'In life too!' agreed Bertie simply, smiling across at Kathy.

Winnie's baby, a boy, was born soon after Kathy's visit to Bertie, and he was glad to hear of this event for his mother's sake as well as Winnie's. It diverted attention from his own affairs and enabled him to get a grip on life. Now that Kathy was irretrievably lost to him, he set his mind on getting back to his unit as quickly as his tardy body would allow.

But it was autumn before he was discharged, and no medical board would pass him fit for military service. Philosophically, Bertie returned to Rose Lodge, the raptures of Hilda, and the welcome routine of the motor trade. He undertook more voluntary work than Hilda felt he should, but he gained in strength and seemed happy enough in his sober way.

The Norths received an invitation to Kathy's splendid wedding in the spring, and suprisingly, Hilda insisted on going, but she went alone. Bender pleaded overwork. Bertie simply stated flatly that he was unable to accompany her. There was a stricken look about Bertie's face, when he told her this, that gave Hilda her first suspicion of his feelings towards Kathy. Not another Howard, surely! She dismissed the thought almost as soon as it had come to life, and dwelt with relief on Kathy's union with another and her probable abode in the northern fastness of Edinburgh. The further away the better, thought Hilda privately. The Howards brought them nothing but trouble, one way or another.

As it happened, Kathy did not move away immediately. Whilst the war still ground on remorselessly, Kathy lived with her parents in the market square and continued nursing. Bertie often saw her as he drove his little A.C. to work in the morning, and his heart turned over as disconcertingly as it had ever done. She looked so pretty and trim in her nurse's uniform, and Bertie envied the lucky patients who would spend their day in her presence.

In the early days of November 1918 it became apparent that, at last, victory was near. After four years of suffering it was hard to believe, but on Monday, November 11th, there were excited murmurs in the streets of Caxley.

'It's true, Mr North,' said an old woman across the counter in his shop. 'The war's over!'

'Who told you that yarn?' quipped Bender. 'The papers don't say so.'

'The paper shop does though,' she retorted. She shook her umbrella at Bender's unbelieving face. 'He's put up a notice saying "Yes! Yes!" that must mean it's true!'

After she had departed Bender made his way out into the drizzling morning. Little knots of people had gathered and were asking questions. A cheer went up as several bell-ringers were seen to run up the steps into St Peter's.

'Where are the flags?' yelled one. As if in answer to his question the cross of St George began to mount the flag staff on top of the church.

'The Post Office should know if it's true,' Bender said to fat Mrs Petty who stopped to get news. He resolved to walk there and make enquiries. Miss Taggerty and young Pringle could cope with slack Monday morning trade for once.

There was no confirmation yet of the rumours, the official at the Post Office said austerely. As soon as anything was known it would be posted publicly. Bender made his way back across the market square. By now there was quite a crowd. Some wag had lashed a Union Jack to Queen Victoria's hand and tied a red, white, and blue bow on her crown. Sep, standing at his shop window, would normally have felt shocked at such sacrilege, but today he was sure Her Majesty would have forgiven this little frivolity had she known the circumstances.

The children began to pour out of school. It was twelve o'clock, and they gathered round the statue to enjoy the fun before racing home to Monday's meagre cold meat or wartime rissoles. At twelve-thirty the suspense was over. A notice was put up in the Post Office window. It said: 'Armistice signed. Hostilities ceased this morning.'

Now Caxley rejoiced. The flag was run up over the Town Hall. The bells of St Peter's rang out and people left their homes to run through the streets to the market square. The crowd joined hands and danced in a gigantic ring round Queen Victoria. Overhead, an aeroplane flew back and forth, very low, over the town, the pilot waving madly to the crowd. Someone had wrapped himself in a Union Jack and rode majestically through the streets on a high old-fashioned bicycle, acknowledging the cheers of the throng.

The town band was gathered hastily and marched through the pouring rain, blowing away at their instruments with gusto. Outside the hospital, an effigy of the Kaiser dangled from the portico, and a bonfire was being prepared for his funeral pyre in the grounds by enthusiastic patients.

Union Jacks waved everywhere. Buttonholes and hair ribbons of red, white, and blue blossomed on all sides. The pouring rain did nothing to dampen the spirits of Caxley folks on their great day. After dark came the greatest thrill of all – the street lamps were lit for the first time for years, and children gaped in amazement at the wonderful sight. Fireworks were let off by the river, and as the rockets soared and swooshed, and the Catherine wheels whirled in dizzy splendour, Caxley celebrated victory with frenzied excitement which lasted till the small hours. Now it was over – the suffering, the parting, the misery! Let all the world rejoice!

But not all could rejoice. Not all could forget. Some like Sep, thankful though they were that the war was over, mourned the loss of a son. Standing outside his shop in the dark market place that night, Sep watched the surging crowds with mingled joy and sorrow. The flags fluttered bravely, the bells rang out, beer flowed freely, singing and laughter echoed through the square. And above all, indomitable and unchanging, Queen Victoria surveyed her people from beneath her beribboned crown. She too, thought Sep, had seen war and victories. She too had lost sons. She would have understood his own mixed feelings.

Poor Jim, dear Jim! But it was no use grieving. Leslie was still spared to him, and Winnie, and the new baby. Kathy too and her husband, and young Robert at large somewhere in the town, and enjoying all the fun with a twelve-year-old's zest for it.

He turned to go in and caught sight of Bertie North limping resolutely along the pavement towards the firework display. What was Bender feeling, Sep wondered as he mounted the stairs? Despite the jubilation in the streets, Sep guessed that there was mourning in many hearts today, not only for a million dead, but for many more damaged in mind and body.

It was going to be hard, thought Sep, to build the new world the papers spoke of so hopefully, but somehow it must be done. Resolutely, Sep looked to the future.

15. *Post-War Troubles*

THE men came back with relief and with expectations of unalloyed bliss. But things were not as simple as that. The first flush of joy necessarily cooled a little. Wives who had enjoyed freedom found the kitchen routine irksome. Children born during their father's absence resented the intrusion of the stranger in their homes. Food was still short and jobs were hard to get. But families shook down together again as well as they could, and it was good to see young men again in the fields and on the farms and working in the shops, and in the market square of Caxley.

About a third of them did not return, and some came back only to succumb to the plague called Spanish influenza which swept the country in 1918 and 1919. Among them, tragically, was Harry Miller so recently returned to his Beech Green farm, covered in honours. Once more Jesse Miller was left to farm alone.

Sep Howard, his Red Cross work having dwindled, threw himself with added concentration into his council duties. He had been made chairman of the local housing committee and found plenty to occupy him, for many new homes were needed for the returning men. Leslie was back in the business and doing well. He and Winnie were living in a small cottage which Sep had bought some years earlier for Edna's mother. Now that the old lady was dead it provided the young couple with an attractive little home, strategically placed at a distance from the parents of both.

The Howards had cheerful letters from Kathy now settled in Edinburgh with the stalwart Henry and expecting their first child. Henry was the only son of a fairly prosperous printer in the city, and Kathy enjoyed some social standing at the local functions. It looked as though Kathy was lost to Caxley for ever, and Bertie tried to persuade himself that it was all for the best.

His father was less quixotic about his circumstances. Young Mr Parker had returned from the war, full of zeal, and was turning North's upside down with his plans for the business. Worse still, from Bender's point of view, his wife and family had joined him and all were to live above the shop in Bender's old premises. It was some comfort to know that his children were numerous and that, for the time being, anyway, he would need all the living accommodation available. At least, thought Bender, his old drawing room would remain intact, and not house dairy equipment and rolls of chicken wire as had once been suggested.

It was in 1921 that Winnie's second child was born. Hilda had begged her to come to Rose Lodge for the confinement, but Winnie preferred to remain at the cottage attended by the local district nurse and a good-natured neighbour. Family affairs were difficult for Leslie and Winnie. The Howards always welcomed them and they visited the market square house frequently, but Bender refused to have Leslie at Rose Lodge although he wanted Winnie as often as she could manage it, and adored his grandchild, Edward. Winnie paid most of her visits home in the afternoon, when Leslie was at work, or called at the shop to see her father whenever she was in town.

A pair of enterprising brothers had started a motorbus service from Caxley to the surrounding villages, after the war, and this proved a blessing. Winnie frequently used it to travel to Caxley, and Edna often hopped on the bus outside her door and paid a surprise visit to her mother's old cottage.

Hilda came less often. It grieved her to see Winnie living in such modest surroundings.

'You can perfectly well afford something better,' she

scolded her daughter. 'Leslie's a partner now, and Howard's is an absolute gold-mine.'

'There's time enough for something bigger when the family grows,' replied Winnie. 'Besides, I love it here, and it's healthier for Edward.'

She did not add that money was not as plentiful as Hilda supposed. Leslie never seemed to have much, despite the modest way they lived, and she too had wondered if Howard's were as flourishing as local people asserted. If so, just where was the money going? It made Winnie uneasy.

All through the long hot summer of 1921 she had plenty of time to think. Leslie had never been a home-lover, and now he seemed to spend most of his evenings out. He pleaded work at the shop, but Winnie wondered. She lay in a deck chair in the shade of the damson tree in the cottage garden and tried to put these tormenting questions out of her mind, as she awaited the birth of the baby.

The heat was overpowering. Day after day of blazing sunshine scorched the grass and turned the chalky lane outside the gate into a white dust bath for the sparrows. Streams dried up, and the Cax shrank to half its size, leaving muddy banks criss-crossed with cracks and smelling abominably.

Water was short everywhere. Wells ran dry, and water carts trundled the lanes doling out a little to each householder. People ran down their paths, buckets in hands, and watched jealously to see that they received as much as their neighbours.

Edward, now a lively four-year-old, grew fractious in the heat and demanded more attention than his unwieldy mother could give him. It was a relief to Winnie when at last her pains began and Leslie took Edward to work with him, as arranged. She knew Edward would be thoroughly spoilt and happy with his grandparents, and she was free to get on with the vital job in hand.

The birth was easy, and by tea-time Leslie was at home again with his new daughter in his arms. She was to be called Joan.

For a few months after the baby's arrival, things seemed to be happier. Leslie was kinder and more thoughtful, and Winnie began to hope that Leslie was beginning to take his family responsibilities more seriously. But, as the autumn approached, his absences from home became more and more frequent. Winnie found herself sitting by the fire, the two children in bed above, alone with her thoughts from six o'clock until eleven or twelve when Leslie returned. He was always in good spirits, with ready and plausible excuses, but Winnie was fast becoming aware that her husband was a glib liar, and that her father, and Bertie too, had known more about his true nature than she had done.

One afternoon, just before Christmas, Hilda was busy decorating the Christmas tree at Rose Lodge. She was alone in the drawing room. On the table beside her was the box of bright baubles which had appeared annually ever since her marriage. Here was the spun glass bird with the long red tail which was Bertie's favourite. She hung it carefully towards the front of the tree. Here was a tiny silver lantern made by Winnie as a child. If only they were all young again! How they had always enjoyed dressing the tree! Now she was doing it alone. She threaded the little lantern on to a dark branch. The broken needles of fir gave out an aroma in the warmth from the crackling fire. At that moment the door opened, and Winnie appeared with the baby in her arms and Edward beside her.

'What a lovely surprise!' cried Hilda. She settled Winnie by the fire. The girl looked cold and shaky. Edward made straight for the box of bright decorations. Hilda removed it hastily, and then began to take off the baby's shawl.

'We'll have tea now, dear,' said Hilda. 'You look tired.

Vera's here this afternoon, polishing the silver ready for Christmas. I'll get her to make it.'

'I've got a lot to tell you, mamma,' said Winnie. Edward's bright eyes were fixed upon her hopefully. 'But little pitchers you know ...'

'Edward, you can have tea with Vera in the kitchen,' said his grandmother promptly. 'Come along, and we'll see her.'

Ten minutes later, while the baby slept on the sofa, and Winnie neglected her tea, the tale unfolded. To Hilda, it came as no great surprise, but she grieved for Winnie telling it with a stony face.

She had taxed Leslie last night with his neglect of her and the children. Without a trace of shame he had admitted that there was another woman and that he fully intended to leave home to live with her.

'His actual words,' said Winnie bitterly, 'were: "I owe it to her. She was always first with me." He goes there today.'

'Very nice!' commented Hilda drily. 'I suppose it's the woman at Bent?'

Winnie nodded. Her hands turned her teacup round and round ceaselessly. A little muscle twitched by her mouth, but her eyes remained dry.

'Well, this has shown him in his true colours,' said Hilda grimly.

'For God's sake don't say "I told you so!",' cried Winnie. 'I don't think I could bear it! The thing is – what happens to me and the children?'

'You come here,' said Hilda promptly.

Winnie shook her head.

'It would never do, mamma, and you know it. Father might not say anything in front of me, but I should know he was thinking about Leslie. It's not fair to either of you. Besides there's not enough room.'

'What would you like to do?' asked Hilda. 'Are you prepared to have him back if he can be persuaded?'

'He won't be. He said so, and he means it.'

There was silence. A robin outside whistled in the grey afternoon and the fire rustled companionably.

'Do the Howards know?' asked Hilda.

'I've no idea. I doubt it. But I shall tell them, of course. Tomorrow probably. I can't face much more today.'

'You must stay the night here. Tomorrow too. For as long as you like, my dear. This is your home.'

'No, mamma, it isn't,' replied Winnie gently. 'The cottage is my home, even if Leslie's left it. I must go back.'

'Not tonight,' said Hilda with all her old authority. 'This has been a terrible shock. We'll look after the children, and you must have an early night.'

'Very well,' agreed Winnie, in a low tone. She passed her hand across her face, with the same gesture as her father's when he was worried and bemused.

Hilda began to stack the tray. Before it was done she looked across at Winnie. The girl lay back, eyes closed, as white as death and as quiet as the baby asleep nearby.

Hilda lifted the tray and crept stealthily from the room.

But the Howards knew already – at least Sep did. At about the same time as Winnie's arrival at Rose Lodge, Sep and Leslie were alone in the bakehouse.

'You may as well know, Dad, that Winnie and I have parted company,' announced Leslie. He was wiping shelves and kept his back carefully towards his father.

Sep stood stock still by the great scrubbed table. Had he heard aright?

'Whose idea is this?' he asked.

'Well, mine I suppose,' said Leslie with assumed lightness.

'Am I to understand,' said Sep thunderously, 'that you are seriously proposing to leave your wife and children?'

Leslie continued to rub at the shelves. For once he was silent.

'Face me!' commanded Sep. Obediently, Leslie turned. He was a child again, caught out in some misdemeanour, and awaiting retribution. Sep, filled with righteous wrath, commanded respect, despite his small stature.

'What lies behind this? What has happened?'

'Well, Winnie and I haven't seen eye to eye for some time. She's been off-hand most of this year. She –'

'She has been carrying a child,' Sep broke in. '*Your* child. What do you expect?'

Leslie flushed. He opened his mouth to speak, but Sep was first.

'There is another woman.' It was a statement not a question. Leslie nodded, eyes cast down.

'The one at Bent?' asked Sep, his voice dangerously calm.

'Yes, dad.'

There was a dreadful silence, broken only by the heavy breathing of the older man. His hands were clenched on the surface of the table.

'Then you did lie to me. I feared it.'

Leslie threw up his head. Now he was angry, with the anger of a cornered animal. He shouted wildly.

'So what? Why shouldn't I lie? I was driven to it, in this bible-thumping house – and so was Jim, if you did but know it! He wasn't the stained-glass saint you tried to make out!'

'You'll do no good trying to blacken your dead brother's name,' cried Sep. 'Answer for yourself! What hold has this woman on you?'

'She's got my child –'

'Winnie's got two of your children.'

'She came first. She always did. We suit each other. And now her husband's left her. I've got to help her.'

Suddenly, the younger man crumpled, slumping on to the wooden stool by the table. Sep, standing, surveyed him grimly.

'You knew your responsibilities before marrying Winne North. You've wrecked her life, and this woman's – and her husband's too. No good ever came of giving way to sin.'

Leslie raised his head from his arms.

'It's too late for chapel talk now,' he said bitterly.

'It's never too late for true repentance,' said Sep gravely. 'You must think again. Don't break up your marriage. Go back to Winnie. She'll forgive you. Break with this woman for good. If she knows there is no chance of seeing you, their marriage may be mended. For pity's sake, Leslie, think about it!'

'I have thought. I will never go back to Winnie. She'd never forgive me. At heart she's her father all over again. I'm starting afresh, and taking Milly with me. I should have married her years ago.'

Sep began to pace the bakehouse.

'I'm not going to discuss it with you further today. Go home and turn over my advice. Think of Edward and Joan. What sort of life will they have without a father? And tomorrow we'll talk again. I shall say nothing to your mother about this.'

Leslie struggled to his feet.

'Whatever you say, dad, will make no difference. I'll see you tomorrow morning as usual. But there's no hope, I tell you.'

'There's always hope,' said Sep soberly, as his son went through the door.

There was little sleep for Sep that night, while Leslie packed his bags in the empty cottage and Winnie tossed and turned under her parents' roof.

The next morning father and son faced each other again. Leslie's expression was mutinous.

'I've nothing to add,' he said with finality. His jaw was set at an obstinate angle.

'But I have,' responded Sep. He leant across the table and spoke firmly. 'If you have decided to go forward with this wickedness, then you must leave the business and leave your home too.'

Leslie looked up, startled.

'I won't have you setting a bad example to the workmen or to young Robert. You know my views. I won't countenance such behaviour. Finish the week here, and meanwhile look for another job.'

'But, dad –' began Leslie.

'I am putting a hundred pounds into your bank account today,' went on Sep. 'Our partnership will be dissolved. You must make your own way. Don't appear here for help if you find yourself in a mess. You've chosen your own road – you must travel it alone.'

Later that evening he had to break the news to Edna and face the expected storm. She could not believe that Leslie had behaved so badly. It would pass. This other woman could be paid off. Why didn't Sep think of it? After all, lots of boys had these passing infatuations. The war had unsettled poor Leslie.

Sep let her ramble wildly on for a time, and then spoke sternly. Leslie was a man. He knew what he was doing. He, as his father, was not prepared to connive in such despicable conduct. He had his duty to Robert, to his wife and to his work people. Leslie must go.

Edna looked up at him with wet eyes. Another thought had flitted through her head.

'What will happen to poor Winnie and darling Edward and the baby? How will they live if you've stopped Leslie's wages? Why should they suffer?'

'I have thought of that,' replied Sep. 'They will be looked after.'

Unable to bear more he made his way upstairs to the peace of the bedroom. In the market square they were erecting the town's Christmas tree. The season of peace and goodwill towards men, thought Sep bitterly, and he had just banished a son!

Beside the tree, dwarfed by its dusky height, Queen Victoria gazed regally across the cobbles.

'She would have approved,' Sep murmured aloud. 'Yes, she would have approved.'

Nevertheless, it was cold comfort.

16. Bertie Finds a Home

CHRISTMAS was a muted affair, for both the Howard and North families. There was the usual visit to church and chapel, the mammoth Christmas dinner, the ritual of the tree at tea time, and for those at Rose Lodge the welcome diversion of Edward's excitement.

On Boxing Day Winnie and the children went to tea in the market square and it was then that she learnt of Sep's generous provision for her family. Leslie's salary would be paid automatically into her bank account. The cottage was hers, rent free, for as long as she cared to make use of it.

Sep explained it all to her in the privacy of the dining room when the rest of the party were playing 'Hunt the Thimble', for Edward's benefit, next door. The table was still littered with the remains of Christmas crackers and tea time debris. The magnificent cake, made by Sep's own hands, towered amid the wreckage, the candles still gave out a faint acrid whiff.

Winnie was greatly touched by this overwhelming generosity, and tried to say so, but Sep would not hear her.

'It's little enough,' he said, 'and my pleasure'.

Winnie broke the news to her parents as soon as she returned home. They too were loud in their praises of Sep's conduct. Secretly, Hilda felt a pang of shame for her past off-handedness towards Sep and Edna. She must do what she could to make amends, she determined.

Bender's first feeling was of great relief. He had been much worried by his responsibilities towards Winnie and her children. She was welcome to make her home with them, though the house would be devilishly cramped, he had to admit. But his salary simply could not be stretched to giving Winnie an allowance, and the thought of Edward's education and Joan's in the years to come had made him shudder. He was on the point of going to Sep and telling him to force his son to pay a weekly maintenance sum. Thank goodness he had never done it! In the face of this liberal open-handedness, Bender was overcome. He had never thought to be beholden to Sep Howard, but he was glad to be, in the circumstances.

It was now that Bertie came forward with his proposal. He had been thinking for some time of buying a house. Now that Mary was growing up, and her hobbies took up a large amount of room, he felt that it was time he provided for himself. Hilda began to protest when he broached the subject, but Bertie was firm.

'Mamma, I have reached the ripe old age of twenty-eight. You were good enough to take me in and look after me when I really needed it. But I've no excuse now. I'm as fit as the rest of you and I should dearly love to have a little place of my own to invite you to whenever you wanted to come.'

Hilda was partly mollified, and when he went on to point out that he would need advice on furnishing his establishment, she began to be quite reconciled to the idea.

Bertie went on to suggest that Winnie might like to housekeep for him. They had always got on well together, and he would do his best to keep a fatherly eye on Edward and Joan. He had been told of a house for sale just off Caxley High Street, with a small garden sloping down to the Cax. It was not far from his work, and would be convenient for Winnie for shopping and visiting her Caxley friends.

'And remember,' continued Bertie, 'young Edward will be starting school in a few months' time. There is plenty of choice in Caxley. He's a good two miles to walk if he stays at the cottage.'

This was perfectly true, and had not occurred to Winnie in her present distraught condition. She liked the idea immensely, and appreciated Bertie's kindness. There would be no quarrelling in the household, she felt sure.

And so it was arranged. The house that Bertie had found was approached from a little lane off the busy High Street. It was a red-brick, four square house, solidly built with good rooms and large windows. It was certainly more commodious than a bachelor would normally choose, and Winnie realized that it had been bought mainly for her benefit.

She told Sep at once about Bertie's proposal and he agreed that it was the best possible arrangement. The cottage would be welcomed by one of his men, he knew, but Winnie's needs had come first.

She had hardly left him before Bender crossed the market square and entered the shop.

'Come through,' said Sep, guessing his errand. The two men settled themselves in Sep's tiny office. It was hardly big enough to house the neat oak desk and the rows of books on the shelves around the walls, but at least they had privacy.

'You know why I'm here, Sep. You're being uncommonly good to our Winnie. It's appreciated, you know. To tell the truth, I couldn't help her much myself, as things are.'

'Say nothing, please. I'm too much ashamed of Leslie's behaviour to talk about it. This is the least I can do. She may be your daughter, Bender, but her children are my grandchildren. I do it for their sakes as much as Winnie's.'

'Ah! It's a bad business!' agreed Bender, shaking his massive head. 'And no hope of patching it up, as far as I can see.'

'Perhaps it's as well,' replied Sep. 'I blinded myself to the boy's faults. I face that now. He'll be no good to any woman, as that poor creature he's with will soon find out. No, I think Winnie's well rid of him.'

'And you've heard of Bertie's plans?'

'Yes, indeed. Winnie's just been here, and I'm all in favour! That boy of yours is solid gold, Bender.'

'He's a good chap,' nodded Bender. 'Bit of an old stick-in-the-mud, I sometimes think, but better that way than the other!'

'Definitely,' replied Sep, with a little chilliness. Bender felt that he may have put his foot in it. He rose hastily.

'Must get back to the shop.' He held out his hand and ground Sep's small one painfully in it.

'Bless you, Sep. We've got every reason to be grateful. Winnie's happiness means a lot to us.'

'I'm glad to be able to help,' said Sep sincerely, putting his damaged hand behind him and opening the door with the other.

He watched the vast figure cross the market place, then hurried back soberly to his duties, well content. For the first time in his life he had been able to succour Bender.

After weeks of occupation by bricklayers, carpenters, plumbers, plasterers, decorators, and their assorted minions, the house was ready and Bertie and Winnie moved in.

The garden was still a tangle of weeds and overgrown plants, but tall tulips peered from the undergrowth in the borders and the lilac was in fine bloom. Bertie strolled about his new kingdom in proud happiness. It was a fine place to own and the neglected garden would give him a rewarding hobby. He paced down the mossy gravel path to the tall hedge at the end. Let into it was a wooden gate, in sore need of painting, which opened on to the tow-path of the winding Cax.

It was this aspect of his property that gave Bertie the

greatest satisfaction. All his life he had loved the river. Its rippling had soothed him to sleep as a boy. In the dark, pain-filled nights of the war, when his absent foot throbbed and leapt as though it were still in the bed with him, he had imagined himself sitting by the shining water, cooling his feet among the waving reeds and the silver bubbles which encrusted them. Its memory had helped to keep him sane in the nightmare world. Now it was here for him to enjoy for the rest of his life. He gazed at it with affection. Here he would saunter in the evenings while the gnats danced above the surface and the swallows skimmed after them. Here he would sit on long hot afternoons listening to the noisy boys splashing in the distance. He might take up fishing seriously. It was a good occupation for a man with a gammy leg and young Edward already had a taste for trout.

He returned to the garden and made his way towards the house. Someone was hanging curtains upstairs and for one wild ecstatic moment he imagined that it was Kathy. If only it could be! But he thrust the thought from him. No use crying for the moon! He was damned lucky to have all this – and dear old Winnie to keep him company.

He waved affectionately to the figure in the window and limped into his own house thankfully.

Thus began a period of great pleasure and tranquillity, for the brother and sister. It gave them both time to recover from the shocks they had received, and to gain strength to enjoy the pleasant familiar world of Caxley again.

They had always been fond of each other. They were both placid and good-natured in temperament, and shared the same circle of friends. Occasionally they went to a concert or spent an evening with neighbours or at Rose Lodge or at Sep's. Vera, their old maid, lived close by, and loved to bring her knitting and sit with the children. To many people in Caxley it seemed a remarkably hum-drum existence. Why on earth didn't they each find a partner, they wondered? Bertie was charming, gentle, and handsome – eminently suited to matrimony, the speculative matrons with daughters told each other. Winnie was free now that her divorce from Leslie had gone through.

The older generation, including the Howards and the Norths, could not help being rather shocked at divorce. To their minds, attuned to good Queen Victoria's proprieties, a woman – even if she were the injured party – was somehow besmirched if she had appeared in the divorce court. Happily, those of Winnie's generation took a more realistic view of her position and sincerely hoped that in time she would find a partner who would appreciate her company and prove a good father to her two attractive children.

There was little news of Leslie and his new wife. They had moved far west into Devon where he was working as a car salesman. With his smart good looks and plausible tongue, Winnie felt he was well equipped to make a success of this career. She never ceased to be thankful that he had gone, and hoped never to set eyes on him again.

Every year that passed made the children dearer to her. Edward attended a small school in the High Street and was to go to Caxley Grammar School when he was nine. One of his friends was Tim Parker, the youngest child of the Parkers at his grandfather's old home.

He had always known the shop well, for he had visited Bender there for as long as he could remember, but he had not been familiar with the premises above until he was invited to play with Tim. From the first, he was enchanted. To stand at the windows of the great drawing room and to look out at the bustle of the market square was a constant joy. There was so much to watch – the cheapjacks, flashing cutlery and crockery, their wives spreading gaudy materials over their buxom arms and doing their best to persuade cautious housewives to part with their money.

And even if it were not market day when the square was gay with stalls, there were always familiar figures to be seen going about their daily affairs. He saw the tall dignified figure of the Town Clerk enter the Town Hall, the vicar running up the steps of St Peter's, the one-legged sweeper wielding his besom broom round the plinth of the Queen's statue. Sometimes he saw his grandfather in his white baker's clothes, or Grandma Howard in one of her pretty hats, tripping across to buy chops for dinner. In sunshine, or rain, winter or summer, the view fascinated him. There was always something happening there. It was as good as a serial story – a story which would never end.

He tried to tell his Uncle Bertie about his feelings, and found a sympathetic listener. Bertie told him old tales of their childhood above the shop, and on his next visit Edward searched for, and found, the scratched initials on the window pane which had resulted in a beating for poor Uncle Bertie. He told the child about the beauties of the old drawing room – the red plush furniture, the sea lavender on the wall brackets, the hissing gas lamps, and Edward longed to be able to go back in time and see its ancient glory.

He was, naturally, more familiar with the Howard's house for here he was one of the family and not just a guest. He adored Sep and Edna, and felt much more at ease with them than with Bender, of whom he was a little afraid. Grandma North he was fond of, but conscious that he must behave 'like a little gentleman'. Ears were inspected, nail-biting was deplored, and his dress had to be immaculate at Rose Lodge. At the baker's house so much was going on that such niceties were overlooked. Here he was happy with the company, but the house itself had not the same power of enchantment for him as the rooms above North's old shop. With a child's disconcerting frankness he said as much to Sep one day.

'It's a lovely house,' agreed Sep gravely. 'And your

grandpa and grandma North always made it very pretty and comfortable. But we have the same view, you know. In fact, I often think there is a better view of the market square from here.'

Edward pondered the point, and lit upon the truth.

'But the sun's wrong. You only get it when it's going down behind the church. Over there, at Tim's, it shines into the rooms from morning till afternoon. That's what makes it so nice.'

Sep agreed again. The child was right. North's aspect was much more favourable than their own. He was amused to see how much the old house meant to the boy. Of course, he had heard all sorts of tales from his mother and uncle about the good old days there and this must lend a certain fascination to the place. But it was not a good thing to dwell too much in the past, thought Sep. A young boy should be living in the present, and looking forward to the future.

'What about giving me a hand in the bakehouse?' asked Sep. The child's eyes shone. He loved the warmth, the fragrance and the bustle as dearly as he loved the square outside. And, who knows? There might be a hot lardy cake or a spiced bun waiting for him.

He danced ahead of Sep towards the treasure house, and Sep, following sedately, recalled with a pang the days when two small boys, now lost to him, had led the same way to happiness.

17. Sep Makes a Decision

It was in the January of 1930 that Bender had his first serious illness. Hilda found him a most refractory patient.

'It's only a chest cold, I tell you,' he wheezed, waving away inhalants, cough sweets and all other panaceas that his poor wife brought. The very idea of calling the doctor sent up his temperature.

'He'll only send me to bed,' he gasped. 'I'm much better off down here by the fire. Don't fuss so, Hilda.'

But after a day or two he had such violent pains in his chest, and his breathing was so laboured that Hilda slipped out of the house and rang up the doctor from a neighbour's. Within an hour Bender was in Caxley Cottage Hospital.

Sep heard about it at dinner time and rang the hospital for news. He was in some discomfort, he was told, but making progress. He would not be allowed visitors for some time.

Sep was deeply shaken. For the next few days he went about his affairs silent and depressed. The market square was not the same without Bender's huge figure in the doorway of North's, and his great laugh sending the pigeons flying. Sep rang Hilda and kept in touch. He did not like to call at the house. Since the Norths had moved he had seldom visited them. Any meeting with Bender had taken place at the shop, or, by chance, in the market place or street.

As soon as Bender was allowed visitors Sep went to see him. It was a cold night of sharp frost, and the railings and lamp posts were hoary with rime. It was good to get inside the warmth of the hospital, despite the reek of disinfectant which always upset Sep's stomach.

Bender looked mountainous in bed. His face against the

pillow had an unnatural pallor which shocked Sep. Clearly, Bender had been very ill indeed. Beside his bed was another visitor, and as Sep approached he saw that it was Jack Tenby. The man rose as Sep came near.

'Don't go, Jack,' said Bender. 'Sit you down, man. I'm allowed two visitors at a time. Stay till Hilda comes.'

He held out a hand to Sep and gripped him with the same old firmness with which Sep was familiar.

'Good to see you, Sep. How's things?'

The three men exchanged news of Caxley friends. Someone had moved, someone else had taken up motor-racing, a third was to be made Mayor next year. The bridge was being repainted. A new bus service had been started to the county town. There was talk of a housing estate in the field behind the park.

Bender listened eagerly to all these topics, but he seemed tired, Sep thought, and when Hilda appeared bearing fruit and flowers, the two men made their farewells and left the hospital together.

The cold air caught their breath as they emerged. Above them the stars were brilliant. Their footsteps rang on the frosty pavement as they descended the gentle slope into the town together.

'How d'you think he looks?' asked Jack Tenby.

'Pretty weak,' admitted Sep.

'I agree. His wife was telling me the other day that the doctor says he should retire.'

They had reached the crossroads where their ways divided and paused beneath the lamp post to continue their conversation. In the light from the gas above them their breath rose in clouds.

'I haven't said anything to Bender about this yet, but I know it will go no further if I tell you about my plans. I'm pulling out of the market place.'

Sep was taken aback.

'For good, do you mean? What's gone wrong?'

'Nothing particularly. It's time I retired myself. It's been thought over and it seems best to sell up all but the original shop. Things aren't easy and are going to get worse. Staffing's a constant headache. I'm not getting any younger. If I collect the cash now and bank it, I reckon I can tick over comfortably until I die. The family's out in the world and it's time my wife and I had a bit of a rest.'

Sep nodded. All this was sensible. But what would Bender feel about it? And what would happen to his old home?

'What about North's?' he asked.

'It'll be put on the market,' replied Tenby. 'Good position like that should help its sale.'

'Jack,' said Sep suddenly, laying a hand on the other's arm, 'let me know when you finally decide. I should like to think about it.'

'I'll do that,' promised Tenby. 'It's going to happen before long. You shall be the first to know my plans.'

He raised a hand and set off at a brisk pace, leaving Sep to gaze at his dwindling figure.

Sep moved off more slowly. He had plenty of food for thought, and he would digest it undisturbed as he walked the streets of Caxley.

How oddly things had turned out! For over a year now Sep had been trying to find new premises in which to expand his thriving business. All Caxley said that Howard's was a gold mine. Only Sep knew how prosperous the business really was. He had saved regularly. His way of life had altered little over the years. As a result of this, and of his foresight and industry, Sep's bank account was extremely satisfactory. It was time that he put some of this money into another business, he decided, and it looked now as if one of his pipe dreams might come true. If North's were to come on the market it would be the perfect place for Howard's restaurant which he and Edna had thought about for so long.

He turned aside down a quiet lane which led to the river. Firelight flickered on the curtains of a cottage. A tabby cat streaked across his path. The smoke from Caxley's chimneys rose straight into the motionless night. Sep seemed to be the only person abroad as he paced along deep in thought.

He could see it all so clearly in his mind's eye. There would be one great room running from front to back on the ground floor, with french windows leading into Bender's garden. A garden had always been one of the highlights of Sep's dream. Here, in the summer, the Caxley folk could eat at little white tables, sipping their coffee or tea and choosing those delectable pastries made at Sep's shop over the way. There had been a need for a good class restaurant in Caxley for many years. Who better to supply it than Sep, who could provide the best cakes and pies in the neighbourhood?

If this property really became his how wonderful it would be! His own premises had been cramped for many years now. True, he had been able to buy the yard next door which belonged to the old herbalist who ran the dusty little shop beside Sep's own. Here he was able to keep the vans and some of his stores. He had often thought about buying out the herbalist, but the property was small and inconvenient, and although old Mr White was in his seventies, and looked as though a puff of wind would blow him away like thistledown, he continued to bumble about among his elixirs and nostrums with remarkable energy for one so frail.

Strangely enough, the possibility of North's ever becoming free had never occurred to Sep when thinking about his restaurant. Somehow, North's belonged to Bender still in Sep's mind, and was inviolate. If it should become his, thought Sep, quickening his pace as he reached the tow path, he would see that Bender's garden was restored as nearly as possible to its former glory. It would be a perfect setting for teas on the sloping lawns with the Cax rippling by.

And what about the house above the restaurant? He and Edna would not want to live there. They were far too comfortable in their own home, and even such a short move would be repugnant to Sep. Would Bender want to return? Would he rebuff any offer of Sep's yet again, if he were to suggest it?

Sep stopped by a willow tree, stretching its skinny arms to the stars above. Bender's waxen face as he had seen it that evening, floated before him. It was no use blinking the fact, thought Sep, suddenly becoming conscious of the icy cold, Bender had not many years before him, either at Rose Lodge or anywhere else. But if it lay in his power, Sep swore to himself, Bender should have his old home again, if he so wished.

And after? Sep turned up his coat collar and set his face towards the market square. Well, if this dream should become reality, then one day, far in the future, Bender's home should go to one of his own – one who would love it as Bender had done.

It should be Edward's.

Sep kept his thought to himself, and said nothing of Tenby's disclosures to Edna or anyone else. Bender made very slow progress, and the crocuses were out before he was allowed to return to Rose Lodge.

He found convalescence even more tedious than hospital life. At least there had been a routine there, a succession of small happenings and a constant stream of people, nurses, doctors, fellow-patients, and visitors. It was too cold to go in the garden. He was forbidden to work in the greenhouse, which was his latest joy, in case he lifted something too heavy or stood too long on his weak legs. Books tired his eyes, radio programmes his ears. Food was a bore, drink was restricted, and smoking too. Visitors were his only distraction, and Hilda welcomed them for it gave her a brief respite from her patient's claims on her time.

Bertie and Winnie and the children called in every day. Occasionally Winnie stayed the night and Bertie took his mother out to friends or for a drive in the countryside to refresh her. She had borne up wonderfully during these tiring months, but to Bertie's eyes she looked years older.

'He frets to get back to the shop,' said Hilda on one of their outings, 'but the doctor won't hear of it yet. I do so wish he would retire. Do try and make him see sense, Bertie.'

'I'll have a word with him when I can,' promised Bertie dutifully.

But there was no need for Bertie to exercise his persuasive powers. When they returned they found that Jack Tenby had called and had told Bender all his plans for the future. So there had been something in the rumours flying round Caxley, thought Bertie.

His father looked pale and shaken.

'That settles it,' he said heavily. 'I'm finished for good now. The old place to be sold, and no job for me even if I could do it.'

Hilda straightened the cushion behind his aching head, and spoke with spirit.

'Don't be so full of self-pity! This is the best news I've heard for a long time. Now perhaps you'll make the best of being a retired man, and stop worrying about that wretched shop.'

'What have I got to look forward to?' asked Bender, half-enjoying his sad plight.

'Looking after me,' said his wife promptly. 'Pottering

about in the greenhouse. Planning the garden for the summer. Helping your grandchildren with their homework. Being a little more welcoming to Mary's boy friends when she brings them home. Dozens of things.'

Despite himself, Bender had to smile.

'Have I been such a trial?' he asked.

'You've been *terrible*!' cried Hilda, with such fervour that Bender laughed aloud, and then began to wheeze. Bertie went forward in alarm, but was waved back vigorously.

'I'm all right, boy. Haven't been so right for weeks! Dammit all, now it's come to it, I believe I'm going to settle back and enjoy my old age!'

It was a month later that Sep called at Rose Lodge – a month that had been hectic for the little baker. He and Edna had talked far into the nights about the restaurant. There had been discussions with the bank, with surveyors, builders, solicitors, and dozens of people concerned in the exchange of property. Meanwhile, his own business had to be carried on, and all the time the problem of broaching the subject to Bender was uppermost in Sep's mind. Now the time had come. The deal was virtually done, and the property his.

He had gone about the affair as discreetly as possible and was confident that Bender had heard nothing. He wanted to break the news himself. It was unthinkable that he should hear of it from any other source.

Hilda let him in with a smile.

'He'll be so glad to see you. He's in the greenhouse watering the plants.'

Sep made his way into the garden. The greenhouse was warm and scented. Little beads of perspiration glistened on Bender's forehead. He put down the watering can and sank on to an upturned wooden box, motioning Sep to do the same.

'Good to see you, Sep. What's the news?'

'I'm not sure how you'll take it. But it's news you're bound to hear before long, and I wanted to be the one to bring it.'

'Well, get on with it then. Is it about Edna? Or has that new baby of Kathy's arrived?'

'Not yet – any day now, I believe. But it's not exactly family affairs I've come to talk about, but business ones.'

'Oh ah!' said Bender, yawning.

He did not seem to be particularly interested. At least, thought Sep, it should not be too great a shock.

'It's about your shop, Bender.'

'Has it gone yet? Jack Tenby said something about an auction if it didn't sell.'

'It has been sold,' said Sep. He ran a finger round the rough rim of a flowerpot, his eyes downcast.

'That's quick work!' commented Bender with more interest. 'Anyone we know bought it?'

'As a matter of fact,' said Sep, looking up from the flowerpot, 'I've bought it.'

There was silence in the heat of the greenhouse, and then Bender took a deep breath.

'Well, I'm damned,' he said softly. Then, leaning forward, he smote Sep's knee with something of his old heartiness.

'Well, don't be so deuced apologetic about it, boy! I'm glad you're having it, and that's the truth! Could have been bought by some sharp lad from London, simply to sell at a profit. Tell me more.'

Sep began. Once started it became easier to tell of his search for premises, for the hope of a restaurant and the general expansion of Howard's. Bender listened intently.

'And the garden?' he asked, when Sep paused to take breath.

'I want to keep it as you used to have it,' said Sep, 'when

the children played there. It was at its best then, I always think.'

'It was,' agreed Bender. 'Tell you what, I'll try and remember how it was we had it, and let you have the plants to set it up again. I'd like to do that for the old place.'

His face was cheerful, and he picked up the watering can again.

'Well, well, well!' he muttered bending over his seedlings. 'So you're going to be the owner of North's!'

He looked across at Sep.

'Ever going to live there?'

'No,' replied Sep. 'Young Parker is going to set up on his own in the High Street. Starting a china shop, evidently, but there's no accommodation there. I've told him he can stay where he is for the time being.'

Bender nodded, and continued his watering. Was this the time, Sep wondered, with a beating heart, to broach the question of Bender's return? Not yet, perhaps. Enough had happened today. He would wait a little.

But Bender forestalled him.

'It's a good house. We had some happy times there, didn't we, Sep? And some rotten ones too, but that's how it goes – and somehow it's only the happy ones we remember, thank God. I wouldn't want to go back there – not for all the tea in China. Too many memories, Sep. Far too many! Hilda and I are better off here.'

He put down the can resolutely.

'But it's good to think of it going to friends, Sep. I'm glad things have turned out this way.'

He opened the door of the greenhouse and gulped the cool air.

'Let's go and get Hilda to give us a cup of tea. Ain't no point in offering you anything stronger, I suppose?'

Wheezing and laughing, he made his way to the house,

relishing the news he had to give his wife. And behind him, thankful in heart, followed Sep.

That night, lying sleepless in bed, Bender pondered on the changes of fortune. Who would have thought, when they were boys together in the rough and tumble of the old National School, that frightened little Sep Howard with holes in his boots would beat him – the cock o' the walk – as he had done?

There was Sep now, hale and hearty while he lay a crock of a man. Sep was a prosperous tradesman, a councillor, a pillar of the chapel, and now the owner of his old home. Not that he grudged him any of it. He'd earned it all, he supposed – funny little old Sep!

Well, that's how it went on life's see-saw, thought Bender philosophically. One went up, while the other went down! Nothing to be done about it, especially when you were as tired as he was. But who would have thought it, eh? Who would have thought it?

He turned his cheek into the plump comfort of his pillow, and fell asleep.

18. What of the Future?

As usual, there were innumerable delays in starting work on Sep's new restaurant. But one windy autumn day the workmen moved in and the sound of picks and shovels was music in Sep's ears.

It was market day, and he watched the first stages of the work to the accompaniment of all the familiar market noises. Cheapjacks yelled, awnings flapped and crackled in the wind, leaves and paper rustled over the cobbles, dogs barked, children screamed, and everywhere there was bustling activity.

Caxley was becoming busier than ever, thought Sep, picking his way through the debris underfoot. Cars and vans streamed along the western side of the square to continue on their way into the High Street. There would be plenty of travellers needing refreshment at the new restaurant, particularly in the summer. By that time it should be going well. There were plenty of local people too who would fill the tables at midday. He had already planned to have a simple three-course luncheon, modestly priced, to suit the time and tastes of the business people nearby. This should provide steady trade for all the year, and he hoped that he would be able to cater for evening functions as well. As Caxley expanded – and it was doing so fast in the early thirties – there should be plenty of scope for Howard's restaurant.

Sep made a daily inspection of the work. Never before had he felt such deep satisfaction in a project. This was building for the future. The thought of Edward living in the house in the years to come filled Sep with joy. The union of the two families, which Bender had refused to recognize in the marriage of Leslie and Winnie, would be assured when Edward took his joint heritage in the property.

One foggy November afternoon Sep returned from his inspection to find the evening paper on the counter as usual. His eye was caught by a photograph of two trains, hideously telescoped, toppling down the side of an embankment. The headline said: 'Scottish Rail Disaster'. Sep read on.

In the dense fog which covered the entire British Isles this morning, an express train from London crashed into the rear of a local train three miles outside Edinburgh. Twenty-four people are known to be dead. It is feared that almost fifty are injured.

It went on to describe the valiant efforts of volunteers who scrambled up the steep embankment to help the victims. Fog and ice hampered rescuers. Survivors were being treated at local hospitals. It was estimated that it would take twenty four hours to clear the wreckage from the track.

A terrible affair, thought Sep. So many other people affected too – wives and mothers, husbands and sons. A number of children were among the dead, for the accident had occurred soon after eight in the morning, when people were going to work and children to school.

The shop bell tinkled, and Jesse Miller came in to buy buns to take back to the farm for tea. Twisting the corners of the paper bag, and asking Jesse about his affairs, Sep forgot the news he had been reading.

It was not until the next day that the Howards learnt that Kathy's Henry, on his way to the printing business, had been killed and now lay in an Edinburgh mortuary with the others so tragically dead.

It was young Robert Howard who escorted Edna to Scotland to comfort Kathy, and to attend the funeral, for Sep could not leave the business or the supervision of the new building.

The news was soon known in Caxley and Sep received many messages of sympathy. Kathy had always been popular, and Henry, so stalwart and handsome, had impressed the neighbourhood during his short time there. It was Winnie who told Bertie the news. His face turned so ashen that she thought that he would faint, but he remained calm and very quiet.

Inwardly he was in turmoil. He would like to have snatched his coat, leapt in the car and headed for Scotland to comfort her. The thought of Kathy in trouble, in tears, lonely and broken, was insupportable. But it could not be. Instead he sat at his desk and wrote, offering all help possible. He would come at once if it were of any assistance. Please let him help in any way possible. He wrote on, feeling all the time how inadequate it was, but the best that he could do in the circumstances.

Kathy's reply arrived in a few days. She was so touched by everyone's kindness, Bertie's particularly, but she was being well looked after. Her mother and Robert were still with her, and Henry's family lived close by and were taking care of everything. She was planning to come to Caxley when the weather improved and looked forward to meeting all her friends again.

This letter, Winnie noticed, was put into Bertie's pocketbook and was carried with him, but she made no comment.

Some days after Robert's and Edna's return, Sep walked up the hill to visit Bender. The shops were beginning to dress their windows for Christmas. Blobs of cotton wool, representing snow flakes, adorned the grocer's, tinsel glittered in the chemist's, and a massive holly wreath was propped tastefully against a grave vase in the local undertaker's. Sep shuddered as he passed. Death was too near just now.

He found Bender sitting in his high-backed winged armchair by the fire. He looked suddenly very old and his massive frame seemed to have shrunk, but his eyes lit up when he saw his visitor and his greeting was as hearty as ever.

'Hilda's down at Winnie's,' said Bender. 'They're making a party frock or some such nonsense for young Joan. She won't be long. Nice to have a bit of company, Sep.'

The two men warmed their feet by the fire. The kettle purred on the trivet. Chrysanthemums scented the firelit room. Hilda had always had the knack of making a house attractive, thought Sep. It was something that Edna had never really managed to do.

'Terrible business of Kathy's,' said Bender. 'I can't tell you how shocked we were to hear it. How's the poor girl getting on? And the children?'

Sep gave him what news he could. The little boy was the hardest one to console – just old enough to understand things. The baby girl was thriving. She should be a great comfort to Kathy. They hoped to see them all in the spring for a long visit. They might even persuade Kathy to stay for good, but she was very attached to Edinburgh and to Henry's people. It was too early to make decisions yet.

Bender listened and nodded, sipping a glass of brandy and water.

'And the shop?' asked Bender, turning the conversation to more hopeful things. Sep's face lit up.

'We've taken down the wall between the shop and the parlour,' began Sep enthusiastically and went on to explain the plans he had for the interior decoration. Bender thought he had never seen him so animated. Howard's restaurant would not lack care and affection, he thought, as he listened to Sep running on.

'You're looking ahead,' he commented when Sep paused for breath, 'and a good thing too! Young Robert will have a fine business to carry on when you want to give up.'

'The business will be his,' agreed Sep, 'but not the house. Our own place will go to him, no doubt.'

'And what about North's?'

'He doesn't know yet,' said Sep slowly, 'but it's to be Edward's.'

A long silence fell. A coal tumbled out of the fire, and Bender replaced it carefully. The tongs shook in his hands, his breathing was laboured. At last he sat back and gazed across at Sep.

'That pleases me more than I can say, Sep. The old house will stay in the family – in *both* our families – after all!'

He picked up his glass again, raised it silently to Sep, and drained it.

It was at that moment they heard a car draw up at the front door and the sound of voices. Hilda hurried into the room followed by Bertie and Edward.

'Bertie brought me back,' said Hilda, when greetings were over, 'and I want him to stay to supper, but he won't.'

'I can't, mamma. I've three business letters to write and young Edward has his Latin prep. to do. We promised Winnie we'd go straight back.'

Hilda looked rather put out, but made no further demur, and Sep watching them all, thought how well Bertie handled his parents. He was, in truth, the head of the family now, with an air of authority which was not entirely hidden by his gentle and affectionate manner. Edward began to make obediently for the door.

'Can I sit in the front, Uncle Bertie? I wish I could drive! I could if it were allowed, you know. Uncle Bertie says he'll let me have a go in a field one day.'

'You must take care –' began Hilda.

'Don't worry, Grandma. A car's easy. I'm going to fly an aeroplane as soon as I get the chance.'

'Really, Edward!' expostulated Hilda, laughing.

'No, I mean it. I've told Uncle Bertie, haven't I? I'm

going into the Air Force, and in the next war I shall be a pilot.'

'Time enough to think of that later,' put in Sep. 'You're only fourteen. You may change your mind.'

'Can I give you a lift?' asked Bertie, turning to Sep.

They made their farewells to Hilda and Bender and went out into the starlit night. An owl was hooting from a nearby garden, and another one answered from the distant common. The scent of a dying bonfire hung in the air. It smelt very wintry, thought Sep, as they drove down the hill to the market square.

Bertie dropped him by St Peter's and drove off. Obeying an impulse, Sep mounted the steps and opened the door. He rarely went inside the church, but was proud of its history and its beauty. It was dimly lit and Sep guessed that the cleaners were somewhere at work. There were sounds of chairs being moved in the vestry at the far end of the church.

Sep sat down in a pew near the door and gazed up at the lofty roof. Tattered flags hung there, relics of the Boer War and earlier wars. He thought of Edward's excitement as he talked of a future war in which he proposed to fly. Would there ever be an end to this misery and wrong thinking? Would the League of Nations really be able to have the last sane word if trouble brewed?

And there certainly was trouble brewing, if the papers were right. Not only between nations, but here on our own doorstep. What would be the result of these desperate hunger marches, some of which Sep had seen himself? It was an affront to human dignity to be without means to live. A man must have work. A man must have hope. What happened if he had neither? Life, thought Sep, chafing his cold fingers, was a succession of problems, and only some of them could be solved by personal effort.

He sighed and rose to his feet. His boots made a loud noise on the tiled floor as he made his way to the door.

Across the market place the lights of his home glowed comfortingly. On his left shone the three great windows of young Mr Parker's drawing room above the gaunt black emptiness of the future Howard's Restaurant.

Warmth suddenly flooded Sep's cold frame. A man could only do so much! He had set his hand to this particular plough and he must continue in the furrow which it made. What use was it to try to set the whole world to rights? He must travel his own insignificant path with constancy and courage. It might not lead to the heights of Olympus, but it should afford him interest, exercise, and happiness as he went along. And, Sep felt sure, there would be joy at the end.

As Sep was crossing the market square to his home, Bertie sat at his desk, pen in hand, and a blank sheet of writing paper before him.

His thoughts were centred on Edward who sat at the table, head bent over an inky exercise book. His dark hair shone in the light from the lamp. His eyes, when he looked up, were just as Bertie remembered Leslie's at the same age. He was going to have the good looks of his father and his grandmother – vivacious, dusky, and devastating.

And so he wanted to fly, mused Bertie! There was no reason on earth why he shouldn't. Bertie thought it was an excellent idea and would do all in his power to help him. Flying was going to develop more rapidly than people imagined. With the world shrinking so fast, surely the nations must settle down amicably together! Edward's calm assumption that there would be another war did not fill Bertie with quite the same horror as it had Sep. Bertie could not believe that the world would go to war again. The memory of 1914–18 was too close. Even now, years after its ending, scenes came back to Bertie as he drifted off to sleep at nights, waking him again. It had been a war to end war.

Thank God, Edward's flying would be used for more constructive ends!

He pulled the blank paper towards him and began to write the neglected letter.

19. *Sep Loses a Friend*

CHRISTMAS came and went. The tree in the market square grew bedraggled, the tinsel in the shop windows tarnished. It was a relief when Twelfth Night came and everything could be tidied away. Down came the brittle holly, the withered mistletoe. Into the rubbish bins went the dusty Christmas cards, the broken baubles, and the turkey bones, and into the cupboards went some unwanted Christmas presents, placed there by the more frugal for future raffles and bazaars.

It grew iron-cold as the New Year broke and little work could be done on the site of the restaurant. Sep did his best to be patient, but it was almost more than he could endure. This was the great year when he would open his new venture. He wanted everything ready by the spring, down to the napkins and the flowers on the tables. From Easter onwards he looked forward to a growing volume of trade. These delays irked Sep sorely.

In the midst of his frustration he heard that Bender was again in hospital with pleurisy. Sep went at once. He was deeply shocked at Bender's appearance. He had not seen him since his visit to Rose Lodge before Christmas. His eyes were sunken, and he moved his head restlessly on the pillow. His hand, as he took Sep's, felt hot and damp. Now there was no vigour in his grip. He could barely speak.

Sep tried to hide his distress, and talked gently of things which he felt might interest the sick man. Bender scarcely seemed to hear him. He began to wheeze alarmingly, and a young nurse hurried towards him and tried to hoist him higher on the pillow.

'Let me,' said Sep, sliding an arm under Bender's shoulders. All his memories of wounded men at Caxley station in wartime flooded back to him.

'You've got a good touch, Sep,' wheezed Bender. 'Got a knack you have. That's better now!'

'That's the spirit!' rallied the young nurse, tucking in the bedclothes with painful vigour. 'Not dead yet, you know!'

'It's not death I'm afraid of,' responded Bender, with a flash of his old spirit, 'but living on – with this dam' pain!'

He put a hand to his side and lay silent for a minute.

'Tell me,' he managed to say at last, 'tell me, Sep, about the shop. The plants are ready in the greenhouse whenever it's fit to put them out in the garden. Hilda'll let you have them. And Sep, the jasmine wants trimming back at that old arbour. Makes a deal of growth every year, that stuff.'

Sep promised to attend to it. Suddenly Bender's eyelids drooped and his head fell back. The nurse hurried forward.

'He's asleep again. I think you'd better leave now, Mr Howard. He's having drugs, you know, to relieve the pain.'

Sep nodded and rose to go. There was something pathetic and defenceless about the sleeping man, a look of the boy that Sep remembered years ago. He stood silent, loth to leave him, loth to turn away.

The nurse touched his arm, and he moved unseeingly towards the door. He knew now, with utter desolation, that he would not look upon Bender's face again.

It was very cold that night. The market square glistened with frost. Icicles hung from the lions' mouths on the old Queen's fountain. The pigeons, roosting on the ledges of the Town Hall, tucked their heads more deeply into their feathers. The stars above were diamond-bright, the air piercingly sharp.

The ward where Bender lay was dim and shadowy. The

young night nurse, on duty, sat at the table at the end near the corridor, a pool of light upon her papers. She shivered in the draught and wrapped her cloak more tightly around her.

It was deathly quiet. Only the sound of laboured breathing, and an occasional moan from the red-blanketed beds, broke the stillness. It was the time of night, as the nurse well knew, when life was at its lowest ebb.

She raised her head, suddenly aware of a change in the ward. Someone, somewhere, had ceased breathing. There was a chill in the air, which was not wholly natural.

Quietly she rose and glided swiftly to Bender's bedside. His eyes were closed, his mouth slightly open in a smile which was infinitely young and gentle. The nurse held the warm wrist and put her ear to the quiet breast.

At last, she straightened herself, crossed Bender's arms and covered his face with the sheet.

The day of Bender's funeral was cold and bright. It happened to be market day, and Sep, as he crossed the bustling square, thought how Bender would have liked that last touch.

St Peter's was crowded with mourners, many of them from the stalls outside. Bender had been known and respected, not only in Caxley, but for many miles around. His great figure was as much a part of the market scene as the bronze statue which dominated the place. Bender was going to be sadly missed.

The church looked very lovely. The candles wavered and flickered – now tall as golden crocuses, now small and round as buttercups, as the breeze caught them. On the coffin, at the chancel steps, a great cross of bronze chrysanthemums glowed in the candlelight. The family mourners sat, straight-backed and sad-faced. Among them, Sep was surprised to see, was young Edward.

Winnie and Bertie had not wanted the children to be

present, feeling that the occasion was too harrowing for them, but Edward had pleaded passionately to be allowed to attend.

'He's my grandfather. I want to be with him till the end,' announced Edward, his mouth stubborn. 'I'm not a child any more. You must let me go.'

Winnie had been about to protest, but Bertie restrained her.

'The boy's right,' he said quietly. 'He's part of the family. Let him take his place.'

And so Edward was the youngest mourner present. Sep and Edna sat towards the back, and Sep couldn't help noticing how old and bent many of the congregation were. It was a shock to realize that he would be seventy in a few years' time and that these people were his and Bender's contemporaries. Did he too look so old, Sep wondered? He did not feel any older than he had when he had first taken his lovely Edna to live in the market square, and together they had worked so hard to build up the business.

And that would not have been possible, thought Sep, his eyes on the coffin, if it had not been for Bender's timely help. He had a debt to him which he could never repay – and it was not only a material debt. His whole life had been inextricably bound up with that of the dead man. Bender's influence upon him had been immeasurable. To say that he would miss him was only stating a tenth of the effect which Bender's passing meant to him.

What was it, Sep mused in the shadowy church, that created the bond between them? They had shared schooldays, manhood, and all the joys, troubles, and setbacks of war and peace. Together they had played their parts in the life of Caxley. The market square had been their stage – the kaleidoscopic background to tragedy and farce. Their families had intermarried, their grandchildren were shared.

But that was not all.

Sep felt for Bender – and always had – a variety of emotions: fear, affection, pity, hero-worship, and, at times, distaste for his ebullience and ruthlessness. Perhaps he could best sum up these mingled feelings as awareness. Whatever happened to Bender affected Sep. Whatever had happened to Sep was measured for him by Bender's possible reaction to it. He could never remember a time when he had been entirely independent of the other man. Bender mattered. What Bender thought of Sep mattered, and reason, principles, codes of conduct – even religion itself – could not entirely guide Sep's actions while Bender lived.

A vital part of Sep had died too when Bender died. From now on the stuff of Sep's life would be woven in more muted hues. The brightest, the strongest, and the most vivid thread in the fabric would be missing.

That afternoon Sep made his way alone to the old garden behind the restaurant. It was sadly neglected. The workmen had trodden down the borders, the lawn was bare and muddy, the shrubs splashed with lime and paint where the men had plied their brushes carelessly.

Sep stood in silence, taking stock. With care, before long, it should look as it did in Bender's day. The grey spiky foliage of pinks still lined the edge of the path. The lilac bushed already showed buds as large and green as peas. Dead seed-pods of irises and lupins made rattling spires above the low growing pansies and periwinkles at their feet. It should all be as it was, vowed Sep, silently surveying the scene of decay.

He made his way to the ancient arbour which was covered with jasmine. It had been made years earlier for Bender's mother to sit in and enjoy the sunshine. Now it was damp and mouldering. Sep sat down on the rickety bench. Bright spots of coral fungus decorated the woodwork, and splashes of bird droppings made white arabesques on the floor. An untidy nest spilt grass and moss from the rustic work at the corners of the doorway. Broken snails' shells surrounding a large flint by the entrance showed where the thrushes used their anvil. The brick floor was slimy and interlaced with vivid lines of green moss and the silver trails of slugs.

It was very tranquil. The river whispered nearby and the overgrown jasmine rustled gently in the little breeze from the water. Tomorrow, thought Sep, he would bring his shears and trim back the waving fronds as Bender had directed.

He rose to go, and then caught sight of something white half-hidden in the shadows under the seat. He bent down to retrieve it and carried it into the dying light of the winter afternoon.

It was a toy boat. It must belong to one of the Parker children, he supposed, but it was exactly like the boat he had once bought for Leslie long ago. Money had been short, he remembered, but the boy had looked at it with such longing in his dark eyes, that Sep had gone into the shop and paid a shilling for the little yacht. How it brought it all back!

Sep stroked the rusty hull, and straightened the crumpled sail. How many generations had sailed their boats on the Cax's placid surface? And how many more would do so in the future?

With the first flush of warmth that he had felt that day, Sep remembered Edward. One day his children – Sep's great-grandchildren – would carry their boats across this now deserted garden and set them hopefully upon the water.

Smiling now, Sep made his way from the peace of the riverside to the noise and confusion of the emerging restaurant. He paused to set the little yacht on the foot of the stairs leading to Bender's old home, where its young owner would find it – safely in harbour.

The short afternoon was rapidly merging into twilight. The stall holders were beginning to pack up now. The children from the marsh were already skimming round the stalls, like hungry swifts, and screaming with much the same shrill excitement. This was the time when the stall holders gave away the leavings, when a battered cabbage or a brown banana or two were tossed to eager hands. Many a prudent Caxley housewife was there too, glad to get a joint or some home-made cheese or butter at half price.

The dust vans were already beginning to collect the litter. The dustmen's brooms, a yard wide, pushed peelings, straw and paper before them. Colour from all over the world was collected and tossed into the waiting vans – squashed oranges from Spain, bruised scarlet tomatoes from Jersey, yellow banana skins from Jamaica, the vibrant purplish-pink tissue paper which had swathed the Italian grapes – all were mingled with the gentler colours of the straw, the walnut shells and the marbled cabbage leaves from the Caxley countryside.

Already the sun had sunk behind St Peter's, where earlier in the day Sep had watched part of his life put quietly away. The air was beginning to grow chilly, and the market people redoubled their efforts and their clamour to get their work finished before nightfall.

Sep turned at his doorway to watch them. For them, it was the end of just another market day. For him, it was the end of an era. He let his eyes roam over the darkening scene. In an hour's time the market folk would have departed – folk as colourful and ephemeral as summer butterflies.

But the market square would remain, solid and enduring, a place of flint and brick, iron and cobbles, shabby and familiar, ugly and beloved. There was no other place quite like it. Caxley life might pulse throughout the network of streets and alleys on each side of the slow-running Cax, but here, in the market square, was the heart of the town.

Here sprang the spirit, here the hope. Sep looked across at the dark shell of Bender's old shop, awaiting its future life, and was comforted.

20. *Hopes Realized*

IN the weeks that followed, Sep's spirits rose. An unusually mild spell gave the workmen a chance to make progress unhindered by frost. If things continued at this pace, he would certainly open on time.

Whenever he could spare a few moments from his own shop, Sep was at the new premises watching with a keen eye all that was being done. He took a particular interest in the remaking of the garden. He knew little about gardening. He had never owned one, and had been too busy to acquire much knowledge of plants and flowers, but Bertie proved to have the North flair for gardening, and he and Edward offered to help in the work.

Bertie's own garden was a constant joy to him. He was very proud of his property and liked to do jobs himself. Since his father's death Winnie was often at Rose Lodge with the children, and Bertie was left undisturbed to enjoy his gardening and his attempts at carpentering and decorating.

Bertie had tried to persuade his mother to make her home with him, but she disliked the idea of becoming dependent upon the next generation. She had always felt a fierce pride in possessions, and would not consider parting with any of the things which made Rose Lodge so dear to her.

'It would break my heart to have to sell, Bertie, and that's what I'd have to do. There simply wouldn't be room for everything, and every single piece means so much to me. That desk of your father's, for instance – and that ugly old flat-iron to hold down his papers! Why, I can't throw that away! And that chair – I used to sit on it to change your nappies, dear. Just the right height for me. No, it can't be done! I shall stop here until I'm too old and doddery to cope, and you must all come and see me as often as you can.'

And so it had been settled. After the first shock of grief had gone, Hilda set about running the house and her many charitable activities with all her old zest and efficiency. She went out and about to friends and relations in Caxley, and delighted in her grandchildren, but she was thankful to settle by her own fireside at Rose Lodge each evening, with all the dear souvenirs of a happy life around her.

Bertie was glad to see her so independent and was relieved too that she need not face the upheaval of another move. His own house was pretty full and he would have had to sacrifice his sitting room to accommodate his mother if she had wanted to come. This he was prepared to do willingly. Winnie had suggested that she should go and live with Hilda, so that she would not be alone, but it was done half-heartedly for she did not want to leave Bertie, and the children were happy in the house. It seemed best to let things go on as they were, and so far everything had gone very smoothly.

Winnie heard from Kathy occasionally. They usually wrote when one of the children had a birthday, and then exchanged news of Caxley and Edinburgh. Kathy had been left comfortably off, and her parents-in-law were kind and understanding. She was beginning to meet people again. Her visit to Caxley was planned to coincide with the opening of Sep's restaurant in April, and she told Winnie that she hoped to stay with her parents for several weeks.

Winnie never suspected the turmoil which went on behind her brother's calm countenance when she read these letters to him. Kathy was never far from Bertie's thoughts. Henry's parents, whom he had never met, he viewed with mixed feelings – gratitude for their care of Kathy and alarm at their solicitude for her future. It sometimes seemed to Bertie that they were busy looking for another handsome

Scot for his Kathy. Would she never return? Should he take the plunge and go north to see her? Natural shyness restrained him. Her loss was so recent. She must be given time to find herself again. He must await her coming to Caxley with all the patience he could muster, and speak to her then. He had nothing to lose: everything – everything in the world – to gain! Bertie watched the calendar as avidly as a homesick schoolboy.

She came soon after Easter, three days before the party to celebrate the opening of Howard's restaurant. Winnie and Bertie were invited to supper the day after her arrival, and as they sat at the great table, waiting for Sep to carve a handsome round of cold beef, Bertie remembered all the other meals he had eaten in this room and with this family. Robert sat now where Jim used to sit. Mary was beside him. Kathy sat opposite, lovelier than ever, but thinner than he remembered. Life had dealt both of them some pretty shrewd knocks, thought Bertie, and they were both a good deal older and more battered than when he had sat there bringing shame upon the Norths by starting to eat his roll before Sep had said grace. Bertie smiled now at the recollection – but how he had smarted then!

Kathy's children were asleep in her old bedroom, but Winnie insisted on creeping up to see them and Bertie went with her. The boy was a Howard, dark and handsome. The baby already displayed a few wisps of auburn hair and the fresh complexion of her Scottish father.

'What do you think of 'em?' asked Sep proudly, when they returned. 'I'm all for having 'em at the party, but Kathy won't hear of it. Everyone else in the family will be there. Seems a pity to me!'

Excitement was in the air. The party was to take place on Saturday evening. The restaurant opened on Monday. All those connected with the building and creation of the new premises were invited. Old Caxley friends and the whole of the Howard family would be present. This grand affair was to start at seven o'clock, and the party would sit down to a superb dinner of Sep's devising at seven thirty.

'Now, do keep an eye on the time, Edward,' begged Winnie at lunch time. He was going fishing with Tim Parker, and when thus engaged the hours flew by unnoticed. 'You must be back by six at the latest to get cleaned up.'

Edward nodded absentmindedly. Uncle Bertie had promised to inquire about a rod in Petter's shop window. Had he done it, asked the boy?

'Sorry, Edward. It slipped my mind. I have to go out this afternoon. I'll call in then. If he's asking a reasonable price you can come in with me later on and see if it suits you.'

Edward's face lit up. The rod he used now had once been Bender's and was sadly the worse for wear. A new one was the height of Edward's ambition. He could scarcely wait to tell Tim the good news.

As Winnie had feared, it was half past six before the boy returned on his bicycle, drenched, muddy, but supremely happy. He was pushed swiftly into the bathroom and exhorted to hurry. Winnie fluttered back and forth between her own room and Joan's, arranging curls, fastening necklaces, and smoothing stockings.

At last the party set off, Edward still damp from his bath, his hair as sleek as a seal's. He gazed in admiration at his uncle's neat figure.

'You've got a new suit!'

'Do you like it?'

'Very much. It makes you look quite young, Uncle Bertie.'

'Thank you, Edward. How do I usually look?'

'Well, not exactly old, but –'

'Middle-aged?'

'That's it! But not in that suit. I suppose it's because it's more up-to-date than your others.'

And with this modified praise, Bertie had to be content.

The restaurant was ablaze with lights, although the evening was bright with sunshine. Sep had chosen white and gold for the interior of his new premises, and vases of daffodils added to the freshness. The tables had been put together to form two long ones down each side of the room with another across the end. The new table linen glistened like a fresh fall of snow, the glass winked like diamonds, the silver reflected the gay colours of the women's frocks and the golden lamps on the tables.

Through the french windows could be seen the green sunlit lawn running down to the Cax. More daffodils nodded here, and a row of scarlet tulips stood erect like guardsmen. The Cax caught the rays of the sun, flashing and sparkling as it wound its way eastward under Bender's rustic bridge. There was no doubt about it, Sep's dream had come true, and this evening he rejoiced in its fulfilment.

The meal was as sumptuous as one might guess with Sep as host, and although he himself drank only lemonade, he saw that his guests were served generously with wine. One of the waiters poured out some sparkling white wine for Edward, unnoticed by his elders, and the boy drank it discreetly. It looked remarkably like Joan's fizzy lemonade across the table, he noticed with considerable complacency, but tasted very much better. This was the life!

He caught sight of his Uncle Bertie at the other end of the table and remembered his fishing rod. He was too far away to call to – he must catch him later. Meanwhile it was enough to sip his wine, and see if he could find room for cheese and biscuits after all the courses he had managed already. He eyed the pyramids of fruit ranged down the tables for dessert. Somehow he doubted if he would have room for fruit as well...

Now his grandfather was standing up to make a speech

– and heavens! – how loudly the people were clapping and cheering him! And how pretty grandma Howard looked tonight in her pink silk frock – as pretty as she looked in the picture Dan Crockford had painted long before Edward was born. Edward leant back in his chair and let the room revolve gently round him, too dizzy and happy to listen to speeches, too bemused to see anyone in focus.

When, finally, the guests moved from the tables and coffee was being served, Edward was obliged to look for the lavatory. His head throbbed so violently that he could not be bothered to seek out the luxurious accommodation provided for the restaurant, but slipped up the familiar stairs to the Parker's bathroom. It was blissfully cool there after the heat and cigar smoke below. Edward splashed his burning face with cold water and began to feel better.

He leant his forehead against the cold window panes and gazed at the market place below. Queen Victoria was bathed in a rosy glow from the setting sun. Her bronze features gleamed as though she had been rubbed with butter. A car or two went by, and a girl on a piebald pony. A man with a violin case hurried into the Corn Exchange. How peaceful it was, thought Edward!

Below him he could hear the hum of the party. He must go back again before he was missed ... back into that strange noisy grown-up world where men smoked and drank wine and clapped his pale little grandfather. It was good to have escaped for a few minutes, to have found a brief refuge in the old familiar quietness above.

But it was good, too, to go back, to join his family, to be one of the Howards and one of the Norths too, to be doubly a man of Caxley. He belonged both upstairs and down in this ancient building.

Swaggering slightly, Edward descended the stairs.

An hour or so later, as the guests were beginning to depart, Edward remembered his fishing rod and looked for his Uncle Bertie.

'He went into the garden,' said his mother. But Edward could not find him there.

'Maybe he stepped into the market place,' suggested Grandma North. There was no sign of him there either.

'Have a piece of crystallized ginger,' advised his sister Joan. 'You can see Uncle Bertie any day. You won't see this gorgeous stuff tomorrow.' Edward shelved the problem of his Uncle Bertie's disappearance and joined his sister at the sweet dish.

At last only a few of the family were left. It was beginning to get dark. The evening star had slid up from the Cax and hung like a jewel on the dusky horizon.

'Cut along home, my boy,' said his grandfather's voice. 'To our place, I mean. Your mother's just gone across. I'll be there in a few minutes.'

Obediently, he set off across the darkening square. A child was filling one of the iron cups with water, and Edward realized how thirsty he was himself. He made his way to the next lion, and pressed the cold button in its head. Out gushed the water from the lion's mouth, giving him the same joy which it had always done.

He let it play over his sticky fingers and hot wrists before filling the cup. He tilted it against his parched mouth and enjoyed the feeling of the drops spilling down his chin. Wine was all right to boast about, but water was the real stuff to drink!

At that moment he heard his grandfather approach and turned to greet him. At the same time he saw Uncle Bertie and Aunt Kathy emerge from the doorway of Howard's Restaurant. How young Uncle Bertie looked tonight! It must be the suit. And how happy! That must be the wine, surmised Edward, unusually sophisticated.

He suddenly remembered his fishing rod.

'Uncle Bertie!' he shouted towards the couple. 'What about my fishing rod? *Uncle Bertie? Uncle Bertie!*'

Sep's hand came down upon his shoulder.

'He doesn't hear me!' protested Edward, trying to break free.

'No, he doesn't,' agreed Sep equably.

The boy stopped struggling and watched the pair making their way towards the river. There was something in their faces that made him aware of great happenings. This was not the time to ask about his fishing rod, it seemed.

He gave a great tired sigh. It had been a long day.

Sep took his wet hand as he had done when he was a little boy. They turned to cross the market square together.

'There's always tomorrow, Edward,' Sep said consolingly. 'Always tomorrow ...'

MORE ABOUT PENGUINS AND PELICANS

'Miss Read' in Penguins

VILLAGE CENTENARY

The village school is a hundred years old and Miss Read, the schoolmistress, is fully occupied trying to recapture the march of those full and busy years under its roof.

But that's not all Miss Read – and Fairacre – have to think about. There's Caxley Spring Festival and the vicar's bees . . . there's house-hunting and holidays . . .

The future stretches invitingly ahead for the whole community.

THE WHITE ROBIN

When a white robin comes to the quiet village of Fairacre, it becomes the focus of nationwide attention.

Nicknamed 'Snowboy', 'Snowball', 'Snowflake', the villagers adopt him as their own. But their pride is short-lived and their hopes brutally dashed to the ground when tragedy strikes. However, bitterness does not last in the hearts of those at Fairacre, and it is not too long before their patience and their faith are rewarded.

'A charming story . . . cannot fail to give joy' – *Yorkshire Post*

Also published

Battles at Thrush Green
The Christmas Mouse
Emily Davis
Fairacre Festival
Farther Afield
The Howards of Caxley
Miss Clare Remembers
News From Thrush Green
Over the Gate
Storm in the Village
Thrush Green
Tyler's Row
Village Diary
Village School
Winter in Thrush Green

and, in a special omnibus edition –

Chronicles of Fairacre
containing:
Village School
Village Diary
Storm in the Village